NIGHT SHIVERS

An Indigo Court Novel, Book 6

YASMINE GALENORN

A Nightqueen Enterprises LLC Publication

Published by Yasmine Galenorn

PO Box 2037, Kirkland WA 98083-2037

NIGHT SHIVERS

An Indigo Court Novel

A Nightqueen Enterprises LLC Publication

Published in the United States of America

ACKNOWLEDGMENTS

When I originally wrote Night's End—the last book in the Indigo Court Series—I truly believed that I was done with it. I really didn't have any more stories to tell in the world. But after leaving it alone for a while, a few gremlins began to nudge my thoughts. Gremlins that started to become ideas. I tried to shake them off because I knew that my publisher really wasn't looking for more Indigo Court books.

In 2014, when I decided to go hybrid, I realized that I didn't *have* to stick to storylines that would have a broad-enough appeal to warrant a new contract. I could take Cicely's world anywhere I wanted. As long as I wrote a good story and wrote true to my characters, I could explore all sorts of avenues. And *that* freedom opened up the proverbial creative floodgates.

So I wrote NIGHT SHIVERS and was pleasantly surprised that there were people out there who still loved the Indigo Court.

2018 Update: Now that I have the entire series back

and am fully indie, if there's enough interest, who knows, maybe I'll have write another story arc of the Indigo Court series!

Thanks to the usual suspects: my husband Samwise who supports me in so many ways. I thank my assistants Andria Holley and Jenn Price. They keep me on track. A loving thank-you to my Galenorn Gang, who make writing a lot more fun with their purrs and meows. Most reverent devotion to Ukko—who rules over the wind and sky, Rauni—queen of the harvest, Tapio—the Hunter in the forest, and Mielikki—goddess of the Woodlands and Dark Fae Queen in her own right, my spiritual guardians. To Brighid, Goddess of poetry and inspiration. And to the Fae—both dark and light—who walk this world beside us, may we see you in the shadows, and in the shimmer of ice. My spiritual grounding keeps me centered and focused.

And thank you to my Moon Stalkers—my fans and my readers, for your support and enthusiasm. You can find me at my Website. To make certain you get all updates on new releases, please sign up for my monthly newsletter. If you write to me snail mail (see web site for address), please enclose a stamped, self-addressed envelope if you would like a reply. Lots of cool promo goodies are available—see web site.

Bright blessings to all,
~the Painted Panther~
~Yasmine Galenorn~

WELCOME TO THE WORLD OF THE INDIGO COURT

Cicely, Queen of Snow and Ice, is slowly getting used to her new role in life. The Vampiric Fae have been conquered and Myst is gone, but now something new is unsettling her kingdom. A ship sails across the Crashing Sea from the Golden Isle with new members for her kingdom, but all of the Sidhe aboard are missing. And the Wilding Fae are appealing to the Fae Queen. Several of their members have vanished, and a large shadowy wolf has been seen on the outskirts of their village. It seems Fenrick, a wolf-shifter and priest of Hel, the frozen goddess of the underworld, is on the loose, trying to usurp control of the Realm of Snow and Ice. Now, Cicely and her friends must face down the monster before he can marshal the ice giants, and destroy the new Queen and her rule.

THE BEGINNING

The new Courts had risen to power, the Queen of Snow and Ice on her frozen throne, and the Queen of Rivers and Rushes in her fiery realm. The time of the Vampiric Fae had passed, and what few were still alive hid themselves, cloaking against discovery. A time of truce between factions was growing—the true vampires of the Crimson Court, the Fae, and the Consortium. Together, the three powers negotiated peace, and looked to creating a world that all could enjoy—including the yummanii —the human-born. But there are always enemies, and there will always be war. And so, a year after Queen Cicely accepted the crown of Snow and Ice, there came to her door the first hint of a new threat—perhaps an even greater one than Myst had presented...

From: *The New Courts of Fae*

CHAPTER ONE

A storm was racing in off the distant ice fields. As I stood at the crest of the hill, I could feel it riding the winds, hard, like a Wind Elemental on an overdose of steroids. The gusts were strong with this one, and the blizzard would be harsh and fierce. I could almost feel a sentience to the storm, as though it were a creature. Hunger drove it. That, and the desire to cover the land in a cloak of white.

I brushed my hair from my face as the wind whipped through, catching up the strands that had strayed from my ponytail. My crown fit snuggly, but it could only do so much in keeping me presentable. *At least I don't have helmet hair,* I thought.

But out here—on the Western Floes by the Crashing Sea—looks didn't matter. Out here, where the ice stretched out over deep oceans of freezing water, survival was the name of the game. And stray hairs were the last thing I was worried about. I was dressed in a thick pair of black jeans. For this journey, I had refused Druise's attempt to get me into my traditional corset top, insisting instead on a heavy layered sweatshirt. The cold wouldn't bother me too much, but I needed to be able to move. Even though I was essentially immortal, if I fell into the azure depths, I could still drown.

Grieve was standing by the edge of the ice sheet we were on, his hand shading his eyes from the gleam of late afternoon light. The sky was silver, with strands of blue streaking through it. The sun never rose, nor shone down with its brilliant beams. The realm of Snow and Ice was illuminated by silver hues, accentuated with pale blue in the morning. At dusk, they faded into a velvety aubergine and then into deep black.

"Do you see anything?" I cautiously skirted the jutting blocks of ice that littered the floe, coming to stand by his side.

He shook his head. "Not yet. I know *The Wave Catcher* was supposed to be arriving at our harbor today."

"Harbor" was a kind word for the makeshift piers we stood next to. The Crashing Sea was as violent as its name, and very few ships ever came over the horizon to dock by our shores. For one thing, most of the ships would have to launch from another realm, coming through a dangerous portal.

"Do you think…will *they* be on it?" I could barely breathe, hoping against hope, but my love softly turned and took my hands in his. His hair hung down his back, spun platinum against his olive skin. His eyes were the black of night, with a thousand stars circling in them.

My love. My Prince. My King. Grieve, my chosen consort.

"Cicely, you know they can't return here. Wrath and Lainule are forever gone from these realms. The minute they crossed into the realm of Snow and Ice they would begin to age and die. They must remain on the Golden Isle, where they will live until they are ready to let go and walk into the mists." He lifted one of my hands and kissed it gently, his razor-sharp teeth grazing my skin. I shivered at his touch.

"I know, but I keep hoping. I miss them." *Miss* was putting it mildly. Every day, I thought about my father, and the former Queen of Rivers and Rushes. They had not only changed my life forever, but had been instrumental to my very existence.

"I know you do. But focus on the positive. The ship is bringing new members for our Court—and for the Court of Rivers and Rushes. New immigrants."

Grieve seemed genuinely excited, and I tried to match his enthusiasm. But the thought of newcomers entering our halls scared the crap out of me. Would they accept me as their queen, given my heritage? I was only half Cambyra Fae—the rest of me was magic-born, regardless of the fact that I had been through a magical transformation.

I was still unsure of my place, and each day brought its own series of accomplishments and setbacks. At least I could speak Cambyra fairly well. I had immersed myself in it, forced Grieve to spend at least an hour a day talking to me in the dialect of the Winter Fae, and though I wasn't entirely skilled, I finally had managed a rudimentary grasp of how the language worked.

An owl hovered overhead, then settled down near us. Shifting—like a blur on the ice—my grandfather straightened up. I flashed him a grateful smile. He knew how nervous I was.

3

"Hunter, I'm glad you made it."

"To see new blood come to our land? I wouldn't miss it, my girl."

"There! I see the ship!" Check, one of my personal bodyguards, pointed out a dark shape riding the swells of the Crashing Sea. As it grew closer, the ship came into focus, ghostly in the mists that boiled along the water. A massive galleon with three masts, the sails were fully unfurled, the wind driving against them with a hard, steady breeze. The wood of *The Wave Catcher* gleamed in the late afternoon, carved from ancient white oaks back on the Golden Isle, the birthplace of the Sidhe.

I strained my eyes, trying to see anyone who might be watching over the railing, but could see no one. There were no figures rushing about, no shouts from the deck. In fact, the silence was downright eerie as the ship slowly approached the edge of the floe. I cocked my head, wondering why the ship was sparkling so brightly.

"Something's wrong. Look at the ice." Grieve leaned toward me, and pointed to the masts. I squinted, realizing he was right. The masts—the railings, the entire ship seemed encased in a layer of ice.

"Reminds me of when the men are out on the Bering Sea on *The Deadliest Catch*." I shook my head. "There's something odd about that ice, but I can't put my finger on what."

" '*Deadliest Catch*'? What are you talking about?"

"Television show. I used to watch it all the time. I can't now that we live here." But I remembered all too well what the ships had looked like, icing up during the freezing storms that hit them. The storms knocked them around like spinning tops, and the men had to get out on

4

the decks and break the ice off before it overloaded the ships and sent them to the bottom of the sea.

"The ice should have capsized her by now, shouldn't it?" I didn't know much about ships, but I *did* know that this wasn't normal.

Grieve shook his head. "No, it shouldn't. The ship came through the mists into our realm. When you really think about it, I doubt if it's been on the waters long enough to become so iced over. The crew should have taken care of it, even so." He motioned to Check. "Take the Queen back a safe distance. The ship is traveling at a good clip and they are showing no signs of slowing down, even though they're almost to the docks."

Check nodded. As usual, I was forced to retreat to the top of the cliff, away from the length of ice that stretched out to form a natural pier. Posts had been frozen into it, with strong ropes to tie down the ships as they eased into the harbor.

As I struggled to see what they were doing, the ship kept its heading: straight at the ice.

My men hesitated at first, then began to back away. Then, as the galleon lurched into port, they turned to run. The ship rammed itself into the edge of the floe. As the two forces met, the scream of wood against ice was excruciating. The ship shrieked, the wood splintering like toothpicks, as the ice—hundreds of meters deep—won the battle, driving like a wedge into the hull of the boat. The destruction echoed around us as the ship shuddered to a halt and then the water began to flow in through the holes in the hull.

My men sprang into action, racing across the ice as the boat began to flounder. Three of them—owl shifters—

transformed and flew up to the deck, shifting back as they landed. It was easier and safer than scaling the ropes, which were swinging from the sides of the hull.

I watched, waiting. We had to get the Sidhe who were aboard safely off the ship. Some were Cambyra—the Shifting Fae. Others were the Sidhe of the Old World, but they were *all* our kinsmen. Fretting, I planned out what we would need. Blankets, food, medical care…but until I knew how many reserves we would need, all I could do was wait and hope that we got everyone off. That nobody would be dragged to the bottom as the ship slowly sank.

The great ship moaned and keened, listing to her starboard side. I tried not to hold my breath, tried not to imagine my men in there, trapped as debris flew every which way. Time passed—I didn't know how long, but finally, the men who went aboard were back at the rails. Another few moments and they took to the air in owl form again, soon landing near us. As they shifted back, one of them—Brazen—stepped forward, bowing low.

"Your Majesty, I regret to inform you that we found no signs of life on board."

I stared at him. "Everyone is *dead*? But how? The ship just hit the ice—surely that couldn't have killed everyone." It didn't make sense. The jolt could have easily knocked some off their feet to maybe hit their heads or break arms and legs, but otherwise…

But Brazen shook his head. "No, Your Majesty. That's not what I meant. There are *no signs of life on board.* There's nobody aboard that ship." He looked just as confused as I felt.

I craned my neck, staring at the shuddering ship. It was starting to list badly. "Are you sure you looked through every deck?" The thought of people trapped, sucked down into the icy depths of the Crashing Sea, made my blood run slow, made the cold suddenly seem more terrifying. I loved the snow and ice and barren fields —they had become my home, but the waters were deadly, even for those of us who lived in the perpetual twilight.

"Yes, we looked in every room. My men are fast and thorough. We would leave no creature behind, Your Majesty. Truly, there are supposed to be over two hundred people aboard that ship. There's nary a one. There are signs of their existence—the ship has food and items aboard. I found the captain's quarters, and one of our men—there he is." He pointed to the ship, where a man emerged to the light. "He stayed to gather what he could. I will go help him now."

As Grieve and I watched, Brazen and another member of the guard managed to catch hold of one of the ropes and hold it taut, allowing the guard still aboard to tie a bundle to it and send it sliding to the icy shore. Then he, too, shifted and flew out of the boat.

Brazen brought the sack of goods to us immediately. I noticed he was cradling something in his arm.

"What's that?"

"It's a cat, Your Majesty. A snow lynx kit." He held it out, and I looked at the baby lynx. It let out a loud mew, one that said, *"I'm hungry, feed me"* or, perhaps, *"Where's my mother?"*

"Only one on board?" I met his eyes.

"I don't know, but Honor might be able to tell us when he gets here." Brazen took the cat from me, though I lingered over its fur. The guard searched through the bag until he came up with a haunch of meat. He tore off bits and pressed them to the young cat's mouth, who eagerly gobbled them up.

Honor landed near us, then transformed back, coming to one knee at my side. "Your Majesty. I brought what I could find in the captain's quarters. The baby lynx was the only creature we found alive on that ship. There was evidence that there were more—at least a litter—but they were nowhere in sight."

I nodded, thinking the kit must have been part of a litter. It was too young to be on its own. "But the Sidhe? All two hundred people coming to join our realms?"

"No sign of them. Nothing but the possessions they brought aboard the boat. No bodies, no skeletons… Nothing to show anybody was piloting the ship at all."

A chill raced through me. Something was dreadfully wrong.

At that moment, a terrible screech sounded—the shriek of breaking wood—as the ice forced its way into the boat, fracturing still more of the wounded hull. I turned, watching the boat begin to keel.

Shaking my head, I forced myself to turn away. "Until we know what happened, I want guards watching over this area. Make certain you set a decent-sized force. We don't want a small scouting party caught unawares. Meanwhile, the lynx…" I looked down at the little kit. Soft, with a snowy coat spotted with black, the cat was beautiful. I leaned down and it gave me a pathetic roar. "I think…you will join His Lordship and me in our chambers. Make certain…" I motioned for Brazen to flip the kit over. I brushed through the fur, then smiled softly. "Make certain this *little girl* is warm and given what she needs and kept calm and happy. If Druise doesn't have the time to take care of her for me, find someone trustworthy. In the meanwhile, we head back to the Barrow. This does not bode well, not in any sense. We have to send word to the Marburry Barrow that their passengers have vanished, and we must alert the Golden Isle that all aboard appear to have been lost somewhere in the mists."

And with that, I turned, my back to the water, as the great ship listed even further. I didn't have the heart to watch it sink.

❋

WE REACHED the Barrow before nightfall, running at full speed over the snow. I was almost as fast as the others now—those born full Cambyra Fae. My initiation into the queenship had seen to that. We ran on top of the ice and snow, leaving no tracks, a silent, swift force gliding by as the afternoon lengthened into dusk.

Once I had taken the throne as Queen of the Snow and Ice, I became almost immune to the cold. And those who made their life with me in this realm also remained untouched by the deep chill. But that didn't mean that a warm hearth wasn't welcome, even though that warmth was a pale shadow of the fires that I had once known.

This entire first year had been a learning experience, and I was frankly surprised that I had made it through with my sanity. There had been so much to learn—and to unlearn.

Druise, my lady's maid, was waiting for me, and she bundled me into a bath right away. We ate dinner late as a matter of course, so she had a snack of my favorite cake ready for me and set the plate on a side table as I gratefully sank into the steaming water. Even though the cold didn't bother me much, the heat from the water seeped into my muscles, easing the knots that had built up during the day. The scent of lilac rose to soothe my senses.

"Where are the new members of the Court, Your Majesty? Did they not come back with you?"

Druise scrubbed my back, careful to avoid wetting my hair so I wouldn't have to dry it before eating. There were so many protocols and rules for decorum that I could barely remember them all. A number of them still grated on me, but I followed them, accepting their presence for what they were: long-standing traditions that I was expected to keep up.

A few things I had managed to have changed. Even those had been hard fought for.

My dress, for example. I refused to wear the heavy, bulky gowns unless it was an official court function. Instead, I wore jeans, though I gave in and wore a corset top with them. That is, except for days like today, when I had been out on a mission. And in a controversial move, I had banned fish from the Eldburry Barrow. I had a severe allergy, so severe I had to carry EpiPens. Anaphylactic to fish and shellfish, because of the danger of assassination via someone triggering my allergy, I had banned both foods from the barrow. Fish was a staple out here in the realm of Snow and Ice, but too bad. If someone wanted to catch a trout and eat it, that was fine, but they could do it away from my home.

It had taken me some time to accept the very concept that someone might want to assassinate me. My cousin Rhiannon, the Queen of Rivers and Rushes—the Summer Queen—felt the same way. We had never expected our lives to work out the way they had. Hell, I hadn't even expected to settle down.

Rhiannon and I were born on the same day, on the Summer Solstice. She greeted the world at daybreak before the sun hit its zenith. I made my appearance at midnight, after the sun entered the waning half of the year. We were fire and ice, amber and jet. And we had both discovered that our fathers had been Cambyra Fae— the Shifting Fae. Rhiannon was born into a snakeshifter clan, and I was *Uwilahsidhe*—an owl shifter. Our mothers were of the magic-born. And now, both of our mothers were dead.

We had been born to take the thrones, and take them we did, after a long, desperate battle against Myst, Queen of the Indigo Court. She had led her people—the Vampiric Fae—on a bloody rampage, determined to bring an unrelenting winter to the outer world, and she had almost succeeded, but we had managed to stop her. Our victory came at a great cost, including many lives, but Myst was dead now, and most of her people, also. A few slipped through the cracks and we hunted them down as best as we could, but with luck, the Indigo Court was nearly extinct. Except for Grieve and me. Grieve would always be part Indigo Court—Myst had turned him. And I —I had been her daughter lifetimes back and my soul still bore the imprint. But we controlled our predatory impulses.

I leaned back in the tub, closing my eyes. "No, Druise, they are not coming."

Druise, a sloe-eyed doe shifter, sounded puzzled. "Is something wrong, Your Majesty?"

I let her brush my hair as I relaxed, the strokes of the

brush easing some of the tension that had built up in my scalp. "To be honest, we don't know what happened. The ship came into port, then hit the edge of the ice floe and began to take on water. Our men went aboard, but…all they found was the lynx."

"She's adorable, Your Majesty. I can take care of her for you—and if need be, I know someone very good with animals who can watch her when I can't." Druise smiled. "I have her tucked in my own room right now, in a bed with a blanket and her food and water."

"Good. I was hoping you would like her. There's something special about her, Druise. You see, she was the only one aboard the ship. There has to be some reason that everybody else vanished but her. We couldn't even find a single rat. There was *nobody* else there. They all seem to have vanished. We're trying to figure out what happened but for now, it's a mystery. Don't say anything. Not until we find the right way to tell people. There are some here who have relatives who were aboard, and we don't want them panicking."

"Of course, Your Majesty."

When Druise finished bathing me, she toweled me off. While I was waiting for her to bring my dress, I brushed my hand across my stomach. I was inked—and each tattoo had a meaning and a life to it. In a life that seemed so long ago, my mother's boyfriend Dane had given me my three tattoos before Krystal decided he was trying to fuck around with me, which he wasn't. But she used every excuse in the world to keep anybody from getting close and that was enough for her to drag us off again, back onto the road. A week later, Dane was dead at the hands of an angry drug pusher.

But his art was brilliant. First, he had given me the belladonna faerie. She peeked out from behind a patch of the flowers on my left breast, shy and yet full of color and joy. The belladonna faerie was connected with another, very short lifetime, I had discovered.

Second, banding both upper arms were matching tattoos of a moon, pierced with a dagger, a stark black work. Owls circled over the moon. That tattoo marked yet another part of my lineage I didn't learn about till I returned to New Forest, WA, to help my aunt and cousin.

Finally, Dane had inked my wolf. The wolf's face stared out at the world from right above my bellybutton, vine work in green, with silver roses and purple skulls sprawling behind him. The vines started on my left thigh, working up across my stomach behind the wolf, then coiling toward the right side of my rib cage. The wolf was my link to Grieve and he had watched over me all of my life, staring out through the wolf's eyes. I lightly pressed my hand against the wolf. Grieve and I were together at last—and that was as it should be.

Druise carried in a formal gown suitable for the evening. Rhiannon and Chatter would be joining us tonight, guests in our frosty realm, and I needed to appear in finery due to the fact that they were the Queen and King of Summer. Cousins we might be, but we were all royalty at this point.

The gown was stunning. Blue as ice, it had an empire waistline, flowing down in layers to kiss the floor. Heavily beaded, the color matched the night sky, the beads shimmering like ice under the soft flicker of the lights.

I glanced up at the lanterns. The Barrow was illuminated by lights containing young Ice Elementals, who gave off a pale blue glow. In the Marburry Barrow, they lit their halls with Fire Elementals. The younglings were not pressed into service, but had volunteered. This gave them time to safely rest and gather strength as they grew into their power.

I slipped on the silver slippers that went with the dress and let Druise sweep my hair back, as she braided a small strand and used it to wrap the rest of my hair into a pony-tail. Jet black, my hair was the opposite of Rhiannon's. My eyes had been green at birth, but during my initiation they had changed and now were frost-covered blue. Rhiannon's hair was brilliant gold. Her eyes had shifted from hazel to gold when she had taken the Summer throne.

I let out a soft sigh as Druise positioned my crown. The circlet was silver, vines that entwined around one another. In the center, they met to wrap around a cabo-chon of black onyx and a teardrop of diamond below that.

"My cousin will be here for dinner. Attend to her lady's maid and make certain she has a good meal, please."

It still seemed odd to have a servant who took care of me so intimately, but I had managed to adjust. At first, I had balked. I didn't like assuming authority over others, but I had come to understand that—for Druise—her job meant everything. It meant her family had standing in the community, it meant that she could afford to help them out. It meant that she had a reason and purpose in life beyond being some scullery maid. It gave her a dignity that I hadn't understood until she explained it to me.

"Yes, Your Majesty." She curtseyed and stood back, motioning for me to stand.

I did, careful not to muss myself. As I turned, she bobbed her head, smiling.

"Do I look all right?"

Though it didn't matter much to me, it did to Druise. My care would reflect on her handiwork, and that—too—was another lesson I had learned. Given my druthers, I would have spent every day in jeans and a tank top. But if I did, my people wouldn't show me the same respect. Here, formality mattered. While I had managed to get them used to seeing me in jeans around the Barrow, more and more, I found myself dressing the part of the queen. It made a difference to them, even though it still felt awkward to me.

"You look ever so lovely, Your Majesty. If you don't mind a suggestion?"

I squinted at myself in the mirror, making sure my makeup wasn't messed. "Of course not. What is it?"

"Your sapphire necklace would look ever so lovely with the dress."

"Let's have it, then." I let her fasten the large, shimmering teardrop around my neck. The pendant hung on a silver chain, and had been an anniversary present from Grieve. We were just past midwinter—which meant we had been married for a year, and Rhiannon and I had been queens for an entire year.

"You were right, it's gorgeous. Is Gri…*His Majesty* ready yet?" Again, I stumbled over the words. But at least this time, I managed to catch myself.

"His Lordship is most certainly ready."

At the sound of Grieve's voice, I whirled around.

There he was, in full Winter regalia. Wearing trousers and tails as black as night, with silver trim, he cut a gorgeous figure. His features were full Cambyra Fae—exotic against the platinum blond of his hair that skimmed his shoulders. Just looking at him made me hungry for his touch. I wanted to draw him to bed, to make love to him, to taste the salt of his sweat, to slide my hands along his skin. With a sigh, I pushed those thoughts away. We didn't have time—not right now.

"You look good enough to eat." I wiggled my eyebrows.

He laughed, his voice sultry and low. "I'll hold you to that promise later." He held out his arms and I slid into his embrace. "Druise, I'm going to kiss my wife now. Why don't you make certain…well…find something to occupy you for a moment."

Giggling, she curtseyed. "Yes, Your Lordship."

As Druise left the room, Grieve kissed me, slow and languorous. His tongue played over mine and my knees went weak as I pressed against him, wanting more. He gently rubbed his cheek against mine, then kissed me again, grazing my lips with his needle-sharp teeth. My breasts were firm against his chest, my nipples chafing as they stiffened against the lace of my bra. Grieve smelled of apples and cinnamon, of the harvest bonfire smoke. Of that hint of snow on the horizon that set one's senses to crackling. I inhaled deeply, wanting to stay in his embrace forever, to feel his lips against mine.

"I love you."

"Cicely, you will always and forever be the only one who owns my heart."

But then, he eased me back as he stared longingly at me. "Unfortunately, we have a full evening. After dinner, we must meet with Strict and the other advisors to figure out what we're going to tell our people about *The Wave*

Catcher. Perhaps by then, our men will know more." He paused. "I brought you a present."

"You don't have to buy me gifts." Grieve was generous, and he often went into New Forest to get things he knew I loved. I appreciated everything he gave me, but I didn't want him to feel like I regretted giving up my old life, even though there was a tiny bit of truth to the thought. There were things I missed that didn't translate to life in the Barrow.

"It's not something I bought." He motioned for me to wait while he went back into the chamber that housed our bed. My dressing room was separate, given the amount of work it took to dress for meals and Court.

When he returned, he had something in his arms. It was the snow lynx kit and she was wearing a beautiful collar. "I had a closer look at her. She strikes me as... gifted. Druise said she's already agreed to watch her. I think, though, instead of staying in Druise's room at night, we will keep her here."

I took the wild cat. She was a handful. Although a kitten, she was the size of a full-grown Maine Coon. We had a number of cats running around the Barrow. I liked them, and the Maine Coons and Norwegian Forest breeds seemed to thrive in the cooler atmosphere.

"So, Grieve and I are your new parents, are we? You came across the great ocean, you know. What happened out there? How did you survive?" I held the kit up, staring into her pale eyes. She stared back at me, and I had the uncanny feeling she understood every word I said. "She's a beauty, that's for sure." And then, the lynx reached out and drew one paw softly across my face, letting out a loud purr, then mewed at me—like a cat, only much louder. It was as if she was saying, *"Of course I'm beautiful."*

"She likes you. Seriously, when we brought her to the Barrow, Check came to find me saying that the moment you left to come to our chambers, she started to cry and she kept it up until just now. The moment we walked into the bedroom, she stopped. It was as if she could sense you were here. What do you want to name her?"

I sat down carefully on the vanity bench and put the purring lynx beside me. She gazed up and, as I looked into her eyes, I realized that she was fixated on me. She reached up and bumped my hand with her head.

"What's your name, pretty one?" As I stared at the lynx, she sneezed, then began licking her paw. "You are so sweet." With a glance at Grieve, I said, "I'm naming her Sweet Pea." I loved the flowers, and something about this little girl made me think of them.

"I have a feeling she's going to grow into something quite unexpected. As to why she survived when no one else on *The Wave Catcher* did, that's anybody's guess." Grieve rubbed her chin. "Sweet Pea it is."

I can tell you something about her, Cicely. Ulean's voice whispered through the slipstream. My Wind Elemental, she was bound to me on a soul level, and had been with me since I was six years old. *She is protected—there is a natural boundary around her that keeps her from being seen or noticed when she's in danger. She has a destiny to play, though what it is, I know not. It is not yet manifest.*

Then perhaps the people aboard The Wave Catcher *were targeted, but she alone remained unseen.*

That could be—I cannot say for sure.

I told Grieve what Ulean had said. "So, she was born

with strong safeguards." Leaning over, I kissed the lynx's head. "Very well, pretty one. You will live with us. But we have to go to dinner. Make yourself comfortable till we get back." I called for Druise and—as she entered the room—held up the kit. "Sweet Pea will be staying here with us. We'll need someone to watch her while we're at dinner. Meanwhile, His Lordship and I will be going down to dinner. Join the staff at the servants' table. Remember what I said about my cousin's maid."

"Yes, Your Majesty." And, with that, Druise took the kit and was off. Grieve offered me his arm and I placed my hand on it. As we headed through our bedroom, then into the hall where Check was waiting to escort us, I wondered where this would all lead.

CHAPTER TWO

The banquet hall was decked out in holly and fir boughs. The floor was white marble, and the heavy dark wood of the table and chairs juxtaposed beautifully against it. At one end of the hall, a huge fireplace lit the room with a fire. Even though it burned fiercely, it barely touched the chill of the air. As we entered, I saw that my cousin and her husband were waiting for us. Another Cambyra Fae, Chatter was Grieve's best friend and had stood by him during our battle against Myst. Unlike Grieve, Chatter had not been turned when Myst overran the Marburry Barrow.

Rhiannon had changed over the past year. Not just her eye color, but her hair color and her stance. A heart-wrenching mistake during her early teens had weighed her down for years, but now the worry of it seemed to have vanished. We were not the women we were and we'd never return to the lives we once led.

When she saw me, her face crinkled into a smile, and she let out a squeak. "Cicely!"

"Rhia!" Ignoring tradition and decorum, I rushed forward and caught her around the waist. We hugged, under the glaring eyes of our advisors. Strict and Edge— brother and sister who were all too much alike—were charged with turning us into proper queens, but they had their hands full.

Finally, I stood back, looking her up and down. We were wearing similar gowns, only hers was as green as mine was blue. She looked fit. Better than fit—there was something about her that shone through. I cocked my head, suspicious, but I didn't want to shout out my thoughts in front of everybody.

I cleared my throat. "Queen Rhiannon, Lord Chatter, welcome to the Eldburry Barrow. We bend our knee to the brilliance of Summer and promise you peace and safety in our realm while you walk under the Winter moon." I stood back and gave a low curtsey as Grieve bowed, courtly and solemn, though I could tell he was suppressing a smile.

Chatter—in as refined a getup as Grieve—caught his eye and the two of them snickered.

Rhiannon curtseyed and Chatter bowed in return.

"The Lord of Summer and I pledge honor to Queen Cicely of the Court of Snow and Ice, and Lord Grieve, her most honored consort and King of the realm. We thank you for the invitation and promise peace from Summer while we are here."

And then, formalities aside, we were in our chairs. I wanted to grab Rhia and go off in a corner. We hadn't seen each other in months now, and I wanted to know if she had heard from Peyton, or Luna, or any of the others —or if there was news of Kaylin, but all that would be talk reserved for private chambers. For now, we would stick to official topics. Which brought us to the ship.

"We have some bad news, I fear." I motioned for the waiters to serve. We were apparently having roast beef and potatoes, and some form of berry compote.

Grieve let out a sigh. "*The Wave Catcher* pulled into port today—or should I say, crashed into the ice floes as it came into the harbor. She took on water and sank."

Chatter set down his fork. "What? How many lost?"

"There's the puzzle. The ship was empty."

"Empty?"

"Yes, the galleon was completely empty save for a young snow lynx. Oh, there had been people aboard, all right—probably the number we were expecting. There were goods and food, but not one person or body to be found except the cat." I pushed my food around on my plate. "We have no clue what happened to them. We must contact the Golden Isle to see if they know what might have happened. We made certain no one went down in the ship, but…"

Rhia's voice was faint as she said, "You don't think…"

I knew what she was about to say because I had been thinking it myself. But it couldn't be. "Myst? No, she's dead. We saw her die. This has to be something else." I frowned. "Remember the stories about the Bermuda Triangle? Do you think it could be something like that?"

Rhia shrugged. "There are enough places in the world where realities intersect. The journal my mother was keeping? The one about the ley lines? I've been studying that, actually. New Forest resides on a huge complex series of ley lines. Think of the town as the epicenter of a Cascadia Fault line of magical energies. I was going to contact Ysandra. The Consortium should know about this."

That was news to me. While the realm of Snow and Ice, and the realm of Rivers and Rushes, existed in different dimensions than New Forest, they both intersected in the Golden Wood. And doorways to other realities were found within the woods. And still others within the two Fae realms. We had managed to find our way to the Court of Dreams, and from there, to the home of the Bat People. All in all, the town of New Forest resided smack-dab in the center of a labyrinthine maze of intersecting dimensions.

"I wonder what her research was for. What do you think she was doing?"

It had been a little over a year and it was still hard for me to talk about Aunt Heather. I knew it had to be even harder for Rhiannon. Together, we had been forced to kill Heather after she was turned by Queen Myst. The sight of my aunt, spread out bloody on the snow beneath us, had been almost more than we could bear. But bear it we did, because if Myst had won New Forest, she would have won the world.

Rhia glanced into my eyes. She let out a long sigh. "I think she was mapping the intersection of dimensions found in the Golden Wood and New Forest. There's no clear statement of that, but looking at her charts, that's the closest thing I can figure out. I'll get you a copy of it. If we both work on it, we'll have twice as much knowledge."

Once again, the fact that we were changing the face of the Fae Courts slammed us in the face. Never before had the Queens of Summer and Winter worked together like

23

this. And Rhia and I were determined that division would not destroy our realms again.

"Good. For now, though, let's just leave it all alone. Our men are examining what they can of the shipwreck. Until their return, let's enjoy the rest of dinner in peace." Grieve shot me a look and I realized that he wanted to keep speculation off the table among the servants.

"Of course." I turned the conversation in a different direction. "So, what news did you have for us? Can you tell me yet?" I stared straight at Rhia, knowing full well she'd know what I was asking. We were too closely bound for her to keep it secret.

She blushed, but ducked her head and nodded. "We made the announcement in the Marburry Barrow yesterday. I'm pregnant."

I jumped up, clapping my hands. "I knew it! I knew that had to be it. Congratulations to you, and to Lord Chatter." What I wanted to do was run around and grab her hands, pulling her close, but I decided it would wait until we were in private chambers. No use giving the servants gossip material.

My wolf tattoo shifted and I sidled a quick look at Grieve. He was smiling and clapping with me, but I saw the light flare in his eyes and knew the news had hit him hard. He wanted to be a father. He wanted us to have a child, and I wanted that too. We had to bring an heir into the world, and I wanted Grieve's children. But I was willing to let it happen in its own time. We had an enormous stretch of time to be together. He needed to quit worrying and let nature take its course.

Grieve seemed to sense my thoughts, because my wolf shifted again and the tension eased. He flashed me a wink.

"My oath brother, I am so happy for you and your Queen. How wonderful." The words were genuine, but still, I could sense a prick of envy behind them.

We finished dinner and then retired into our private chambers, along with Strict and Edge. The guards stayed outside.

Once the heavy doors were shut, we relaxed. Crowns could never come off, not in any public setting, but we all dropped into our seats. Rhia lifted one of her feet, groaning.

"My feet are swollen, my hands are swollen…everything feels bloated."

"How far along are you?" I moved to her side, motioning for her to lie back on the sofa. "Rest. I'll rub your feet."

She gratefully reclined, closing her eyes. "Thank you. Only four months. I think this will be a boy. I just have a feeling. I always expected to have a girl first, but you never know, I guess."

I took her feet in hand, rubbing them, gently compressing her swollen ankles. Rhia had always been tall and wisp-thin, but since our transformations into Fae Queens, she had grown more sturdy, and I had no worries about her handling the pregnancy.

Strict cleared his throat. "Your Majesty, about the shipwreck—what should I tell the populace? Some of them are waiting for family members."

I let out a short sigh. "I hate to bring it up, but we'd better discuss this now. Rhia, I think both Courts should release a joint statement, because some of those Fae were bound for the Marburry Barrow. If I release the news now, or you release it before I do, then word will spread and whoever is slow in getting the word out will be inundated with pleas for information."

She nodded. "I think you're right. What will we say?"

I turned to Strict. "This is your department. Why don't you and Edge draft an announcement, we'll okay it, then on the stroke of midnight, both Barrows can release the news. It's obvious something is wrong since we didn't come home with anybody in tow."

Strict bowed. "As you will, Your Majesty." He withdrew with his sister to the side of the room and they began their work.

Meanwhile, I went back to rubbing my cousin's feet.

She snuggled back against the cushions. "Did you ever think, in a million years, this is how we would end up?" She closed her eyes and murmured softly as I worked the tension out of her toes.

I laughed. "Not so much. Hell, Krystal dragged me to hell and back. Honestly, when Heather called me, asking me to return to New Forest, I was just hoping to kick back in the only house that ever felt like home to me. I was just hoping to stay in one place for more than a few months. I never expected *anything* like this."

"I may have grown up in the Veil House, but I never envisioned this, either."

I paused, lightly kneading her calves. "Sometimes, it's almost too much. I went from street urchin to Faerie Queen. Some nights I wake up, scared that I'll have to pack up and head out again. But those days are over, aren't they? The Faerie-tale ending only led to a new beginning. I found my prince, and he came attached with a kingdom and all the accompanying responsibilities."

In the months since we had fought Myst's armies, I

had tried to relax, to adapt. But the intensity of that battle, the bloodshed and the death and the loss…it still invaded my dreams. There were nights when I dreaded closing my eyes because I would slip into a pale somnolence, unable to fully sleep, but instead, I would relive the carnage, the memories vivid and fierce.

"Sometimes, I think…if I hadn't come back, none of this…Myst…it wouldn't have happened." I seldom broached that thought. For one thing, it terrified me to think maybe I was the cause of the war. But logically, I knew that wasn't the truth. Logic and emotion waged war, though, and logic wasn't always the frontrunner.

"No. We would have just lost. She had already made incursions. She had taken over the Courts of Rivers and Rushes, and that of Snow and Ice. She was making inroads on New Forest, and she would have ravaged her way through the land with no one to stop her." With a sigh, Rhia pushed herself to a seated position again. She gave me a light kiss. "Thank you for my foot rub. I needed it. But I think we'd best be going home, if Strict and Edge have finished."

Speak of the devil, the pair returned to our side, document in hand. "We have a short statement here, Your Majesties…if we may read it?"

Grieve and Chatter stopped whatever conversation they were having and joined us.

I nodded at Strict. "Proceed, please."

"Very well." He held out the paper.

"IT IS WITH CONCERN THAT THE COURT OF SNOW AND ICE REGRETS TO INFORM YOU THAT THE WAVE CATCHER, THE SHIP

BOUND FROM THE GOLDEN ISLE, HAS SUNK OFF THE SHORE OF THE CRASHING SEA. A THOROUGH EXAMINATION HAS BEEN MADE. IT HAS BEEN NOTED THAT NO SIGNS OF LIFE WERE FOUND. THERE WERE INDICATIONS THAT THE CREW AND PASSENGERS HAD BEEN ABOARD, BUT BY THE TIME THE SHIP REACHED THE SHORE, ANY AND ALL PERSONNEL HAD VANISHED. WE CURRENTLY HAVE NO OFFICIAL EXPLANATION FOR THEIR DISAP-PEARANCE. A JOINT INVESTIGATION IS BEING LAUNCHED BY THE COURTS OF SUMMER AND WINTER. PLEASE LIMIT SPECULATION AS TO WHAT HAS HAPPENED UNTIL WE HAVE SUBSTANTIATED EVIDENCE ON WHICH TO PROCEED. AS SOON AS WE HAVE FURTHER INFORMATION, WE WILL ANNOUNCE OUR FINDINGS."

I THOUGHT OVER THE WORDING. Apologetic without taking responsibility—very apt and very important. "It works. Please make certain that the Court of Summer has a copy to take home with them."

I stood, wishing that Rhia and Chatter could stay, but a knock on the door forestalled any more discussion of the issue. Strict answered and ushered Check into the room.

My personal guard saluted and gave us a quick, stiff bow. I had come to rely on him for so much. He was loyal to the core, and he never failed to give his opinion, though always with respect, when I needed it. Now, he had a perplexed look on his face.

"What's wrong, Check?" I knew that look. It meant that something had happened and he wasn't sure whether it was something he should bother me about.

"One of the Wilding Fae is waiting to see you, Your Majesty. The Snow Hag."

I blinked. I hadn't seen the Snow Hag in months. The

Wilding Fae had managed to settle into the Court of Snow and Ice and were slowly but surely making their home here. They were an odd lot, far more ancient than any of the other Fae, and all were unique, with odd manners and powers that—I suspected—far outstripped our own.

"Please show her in." I arranged my gown as Rhia slid her shoes back on.

The Wilding Fae had helped us during Myst's siege, but they were aloof and insular, and they tended to stick to themselves even though they had reached out to me. I honored their solitary natures, and seldom required they visit the Barrow. And the Snow Hag…she had been invaluable to us. And she had become a friend—of sorts —to me.

As Check ushered her in, I stood as a sign of honor. So did Rhia, Grieve, and Chatter. We all recognized just how much she had done for us.

She entered and, once again, I was struck by how disparate her looks were from the power behind those cunning eyes. Short, the Snow Hag wore a patchwork dress that trailed behind her. She might as well have dreads, her hair was so matted. Her face was a topo- graphical map of her life, and her body was slight—thin to the point of being frighteningly gaunt. She was gnarled, and hunched. One of her teeth curved up like a fang, giving her an overbite from the bottom lip.

"A Queen of Ice does not make a guest wait long at her door. The honor is welcomed." She swept into a deep curtsey, bending one knee almost to the floor.

All the Wilding Fae spoke in riddles, and it was important to match their cadence. It had taken me some time, but I finally had the pattern down…for the most part.

"A guest such as one of the Wilding Fae must never be overlooked—especially one so welcome in the Court's chambers." I inclined my head.

"Pleasantries are indeed pleasant, and a guest from the Wilding Fae might well bid greetings and respect to a Queen's guests." Once again, the odd cadence flowed off her tongue like smooth honey.

Rhia, Grieve, and Chatter gave her solemn nods, smiling as they did so.

"What may a Queen do for a guest this ice-filled evening?"

The Snow Hag cocked her head, her eyes twinkling. She winked, very soft and quick, but it was still a recognition seldom offered by their kind. "Perhaps a Queen might listen to a tale of fear and worry from her subjects."

"A Queen would bid her guest to rest, and to speak freely."

She sat in one of the chairs cautiously, as though not used to the comforts of our Barrow. I wasn't sure what her home was like. Hell, to be honest, I had no clue where the Wilding Fae actually lived. They never invited anyone to their homes, and I wasn't entirely sure they were fully within our plane of existence.

"The Wilding Fae have been attacked. There might be fear in the heart of a guest about the attacker. There might be fear that the attacker may be as fiercesome as a departed enemy shared by many."

I caught my breath. Twice now, the fear that Myst might be returning had been brought up. Two times too many for one day.

"A guest would please tell a Queen what happened to those attacked."

The Snow Hag inclined her head. "One of the Wilding Fae, and yet a second, were found murdered. It is surmised the killing happened this morning, but circumstances only brought their deaths to light during the quietude of dusk. There may have been a search, but no sign found of who chose to attack. The bodies might have been torn to bits. Indeed, a guest might have memories of the Vampiric Fae because of the savagery of the attack." The singsong of her cadence was mesmerizing, but as her words drifted to a stop, a cold chill settled over the room.

I froze. Myst was dead. It couldn't be her, could it? Yes, the Vampiric Fae were still out there, but in raggle-taggle groups, hiding in order to save their lives. They were in no shape to launch an attack, especially against the Wilding Fae.

Or could they have banded together? It had been a year, after all.

Ulean...are you here?

I am here. Fear not. What is wrong, Cicely?

I ran down the situation for her—I always thought of Ulean as a "she" even though she wasn't really any gender.

Do you think that the Vampiric Fae could be massing again, under a new ruler? Or...I returned from a past life to find Grieve. You don't think Myst may be back?

I do not sense her—no, but there is a shadow overreaching the area, and I have no idea what it is. Let me search and find out what I can. As for Myst, I do not think she will ever return. I could be wrong, but it would take a far greater power than a year's time out of body for her to be able to regroup after you destroyed her heartstone.

31

And with that, Ulean swept out of the room.

I turned to the Snow Hag. "A Queen may send out a search party to find out what she can glean. She may also send soldiers home with a guest, to examine the tragedy. Is there anything else a Queen might do for a guest, to ease the loss for the Wilding Fae?"

A moment's pause, then another.

Finally—"A Queen may have given hope to a guest, for the guest is feeling weary this evening. A guest might be nearing the long last ends of her life, when weariness comes easily, and such a guest may tire from little exertion."

A sharp pain hit my chest. We had lost so many in the war against Myst. I truly liked the Snow Hag, and to lose her, too…

"Please tell a Queen if there is a way she can help a guest to ease her pain and weariness. To heal what is wounded and worn out?" I knew the answer to that one already, but I had to ask, had to hope. Always, always strive for hope.

The Snow Hag smiled gently, then, and surprised me by reaching out a hand. I slowly took her fingers in mine, surprised to find her so warm against my own flesh.

"A Queen may help by simply asking. By being the friend she is. And a guest honors and values the offer and hope. A Queen should be at peace. Death is not coming quite yet to claim an old body, though it is sniffing at the outskirts of the village, and will eventually come riding through. Everything must perish, in its own time. A Queen will never be able to stave off the turn of the wheel —to do so is simply not within any grasp." And she let go of my hand, cocking her head to the side again.

I understood her. She was dying and nothing anyone could do would stop the eventuality. How long she had, who could say? I swallowed hard, wanting to cry. I hadn't realized just how much I liked the crafty old woman. I didn't have a clear grasp on the nature of the Wilding Fae yet, and I didn't know if I ever would, but I knew they were a rare breed, and each one was a unique part of their culture.

"A Queen understands what a guest is saying. And that Queen would have that guest know how very much this saddens her heart, and how very special that guest is to the Court of Snow and Ice. Several of the Queen's soldiers will go with a guest whenever she is ready, to examine the losses."

The Snow Hag gazed into my eyes, holding my attention. She was ancient, old beyond the trees in the Golden Wood, old beyond the formation of the country, perhaps even predating the first humans who walked on this land. But she was right…everything came to an end. Even the Sidhe. While I could die through being killed, my life stretched out to the possibility of thousands of years. But eventually the Sidhe faded if they did not die and they became one with the world to the point of being walking, breathing memories.

I let out a long sigh as the Snow Hag stood.

She said nothing as I instructed Check to send several of our men with her, but merely turned and walked out the door, still silent.

I bit my lip, suddenly very tired. With *The Wave Catcher*'s sudden sinking, the disappearance of the Fae on board, and now this, the day had been exhausting. I settled back on the sofa and Rhia sat beside me, wrapping her arms around my shoulders.

"It will be all right. Everything will work out."

"There will never be an end to it, will there? There will always be some terror, some mystery to throw life into turmoil. I thought when I returned to New Forest, I could put all of that behind me. That maybe, I could just settle in and breathe. I spent my life running from one problem to another, and I hoped…" I stopped, a sudden realization sweeping over me. "This *is* life, isn't it? I always blamed Krystal for the drama and the worry, but no matter where you go, no matter who you are, or where you live…there will always be some disruption, won't there?"

Strict had edged over and now, he sat down in a chair opposite me. He was as his name implied—definitely strict, but he also had an understanding nature that had come out more during the past year. Now, he cleared his throat and leaned forward.

"Your Majesty, no matter where you go, or who you are with, life will always throw curve balls—as the yummanii put it. There is no safe haven where you can hide away from the world. In fact, I would say the only place to escape what life has to throw at you is in death."

And there it was. Black and white. There was no happily-ever-after because, until you died, *after* always kept coming. Even during moments of great happiness, something would shift to tear down the joy. And in sorrow, joy would lift us up again. A continual cycle.

"I suppose you're right. I kind of hoped that once we were married and took the thrones, that once Myst was dead, everything would be okay, and life would play out without any more issues. I guess that makes me a fool."

"It makes you a dreamer, is what it makes you." Rhia stretched and yawned. "I thought I was the optimist of the group, but honestly, as screwed up as our lives have been —yours more than mine, I grant you that—I think…I think I'm happy things have happened the way they have. I miss my mother, but look at what I have."

I kissed her softly on the cheek. "You're right, of course. Life will keep coming, and it brings both sorrow but also joy. I guess I'll learn as I go. You journey safely home. My men will see you to the Twin Hollies where the portal lies. Do you have security waiting on the other side?"

She nodded. "We do. When we get home, Edge will make the announcement about the ship. I figure, at midnight, respectively?"

"Midnight it is, then." Both Rhiannon and I kept clocks in the Barrows. Even though time ran on a different scale here, it gave us some sense of what time and day it was in the outer worlds, and provided us with a frame of reference.

As the guards escorted them out into the hall and toward the front of the Barrow, I longed to go with them, to wave good-bye, but that would break decorum.

I turned to Grieve as the door shut behind them. "So, Rhiannon and Chatter are going to have a baby."

"And they already have the tyke they adopted." Grieve's voice held a wistful note, and I wanted to hug him, to promise that I would get pregnant right away. But the truth was, I had no clue why we weren't there yet. It had been almost a year. A little part of me worried that, perhaps, when Myst had turned Grieve, it had changed something in his body that might interfere with our abilities to conceive. I had spoken about it to one of our personal healers, and she was looking into the subject. Until she had an answer—or the hope of an answer—I didn't want to bring it up to Grieve, though. I didn't want to make him feel bad. For all I knew, *my* body wasn't being cooperative. I was waiting on test results for that, too.

As if reading my mind, Grieve held out his hand. "Why don't we go work on the issue?" A light shimmered in his eyes, and my body burned under his scrutiny.

"I would like that." I turned to Strict. "Make the announcement when the clock shows midnight. Field all questions for us till morning. Make sure the men going with the Snow Hag return. If there's a problem, rouse us from our chamber."

And with that, Grieve and I headed toward our bedroom, Check following behind us to make certain we got there safely.

❋

It had taken some time for me to be comfortable with the constant security force surrounding me, but now it felt second nature. I finally had come to understand that a part of my discomfort came from the misplaced feeling that it was self-indulgent. Maybe even a little arrogant. But as the realization that assassination attempts were an actual threat hit home, I quickly shifted gears. Having bodyguards wasn't self-important. The fact was that I *was* a queen, and that meant I held vast power in my hands. And *that* meant that there would always be someone wanting to either co-opt that power, or to oust me from the throne because they didn't like the way I did things.

As we reached the door of our bedchamber, Check motioned for us to wait with Shelter while he went in. This was our routine every night. The pair would escort us to our chamber, and Check would scout the bedroom and bath for any signs of problems. Druise would be waiting inside. Then, Check would return and we would go in. Druise would undress me, brush my hair, and then she would go to her small room, which was right next to ours. Check and Shelter would be on guard during the first hours of the night, then trade off with Fearless and Wonder partway through the night.

As Druise bid us good night, I turned to Grieve. I was wearing my robe, but now I let it slide off my shoulders to drop to the floor. Grieve's eyelashes fluttered softly as he looked at me, then his clothes were gone. Full Cambyra Fae had the ability to dress as they would at a moment's thought, though they dressed for their stations. They could be wearing the finest robes in the land, then the next second, be thoroughly naked.

Grieve leaned against one of the posters on the bed, lean and muscled, his skin gleaming with a soft olive glow. His hair draped over his shoulders. With his dark, star-dappled eyes, he looked altogether alien and yet, totally familiar. And he wanted me.

I let my gaze trail up his body. Grieve was hard, his cock thick and firm. I couldn't tear my gaze away—just being near him drove me out of my mind. He was like a heady wine, intoxicating. I trailed my left hand over my body, lingering on my breasts as I stroked myself with my right.

"Don't stop." Grieve's voice was strangled as he watched me.

I slid one finger over my clit and swirled it gently, letting out a soft moan as I pinched my left nipple hard. Shuddering, I shifted my hips to one side.

Softly, my words a whisper—"You know what I want."

"Tell me what you want. I want to hear you say it." He took one slow step forward.

"I want you to fuck me. I want your tongue driving me wild. I want you to throw me on the bed and drive your cock deep inside me. I want you to fuck me till I scream, to fill me up so there's no room for anything else." I let out a slight sob—Grieve always affected me this way. He was my match, and sometimes it was almost too much to bear.

With a low growl, he was suddenly in front of me. He seized me, carrying me to the bed where he tossed me on the soft pile of quilts and covers. I stared at the ceiling, a sparkling mosaic of iolite, sapphire, amethyst, and clear quartz. They glowed, creating the sense of being under the stars. The dark yew of the furniture was polished to a high sheen, creating a heavy Old World feel. The four-poster bed stood on a cobblestone floor, a tapestry to protect our feet.

Now, Grieve was on the bed, looming over me, a feral smile on his face. When he lowered his lips to my breast, I gasped. I wrapped my legs around his waist, pulling him into me, into my core and center. As his shaft penetrated my sex, I moaned. He was thick and wide, and as he drove himself deeper, I let out a shriek and squirmed beneath him.

"Fuck me, please, fuck me."

I rose to meet him as he plunged, every thrust stoking

the fire, every shift and swivel of his hips forcing a cry from my lips. My need grew into a blazing fire, overshadowing anything else in my world, and I slid into the haze of desire. And then, he slipped a hand between us and reached down. As he stroked me, rough and hard, the pain shot through me, mingling with the pleasure, and I came —sobbing and laughing as the floodgates opened and all my worry and concern and responsibility ceased to exist.

There was only Grieve, and only me, and we were the only people to exist in this one moment, captured in the rush of orgasm. As the wave pushed me higher, he began to thrust faster, and then—arching his back—he cried out, calling my name. I came again, this time in a shower of stars and snow. Everything stood still for a moment, and then—with a soft shift, he began to thrust gently, loving me with his body, loving me with the soft murmur of his words, and we continued, long into the night, weaving a world with our bodies, a world where only the two of us existed. Where missing passengers and vicious enemies vanished from thought, and love and passion were the sun and the moon.

CHAPTER THREE

Morning came all too early, and earlier than usual when Sweet Pea landed on the bed and started licking my face. I laughed, blinking, as I forced myself to sit up. She rolled over for a belly rub and I wondered how long her kittenish nature would last.

As my head cleared, I found myself wondering what my men had found out at the village of the Wilding Fae. I realized I didn't even know if they had named their village—and while it seemed a small thing in the scheme of things, it was a detail that I should know. Strict's constant lessons were drummed into my head, and one of the most prominent was, "A Queen shall always know the details of her kingdom—and she will always know how the mood of her people runs."

I rose and tugged on the long, velvet rope pull. Within less than a minute, Druise tapped quietly on the door and then entered. She was ready—always waiting for me.

"Your Majesty, good morning."

"Morning, Druise. Will you take Sweet Pea to be fed and cared for."

"Yes, Your Majesty. Are you ready to bathe?" She moved toward the bathroom.

"Yes, please." When we first took over the Eldburry Barrow, I had insisted that the Cambyra Fae responsible for outfitting the structure of the place rig up a bathtub that provided instant hot water. I didn't care whether it was via magic or they had to import technology from the outer world. Two things I refused to relinquish were a bathtub and a flush toilet. Three, actually: an espresso machine. I wasn't sure how they had managed it, but they had come through on all of them.

Druise carried the lynx away to her room, then returned to draw my bath as I pushed my arms through my robe. I could smell the lemon bath salts.

Grieve was still asleep. He snored, though not loudly, and looked very much like a little boy as he curled under the covers. I leaned over to kiss him on the forehead, then quietly padded into the bathroom, where I hung up my robe and climbed into the big claw-foot tub.

"What would you wear this morning, Your Majesty?" Druise deftly placed a bath cushion behind my neck and handed me a soft cloth and some soap. I bought my soaps and bath gels in New Forest, a holdover from my old life.

With a glance at her, I began lathering up. "I don't know yet. Druise, do you think it's odd for me to hold onto parts of my old life? The bath gels and espresso and…other things." I missed my car most of all. Books, I could easily bring into the realm. The same with food and trinkets. Movies—not so easy, so now and then I went into New Forest to hang out with Peyton, a good friend who had helped destroy Myst, and we would spend all afternoon watching movies and I would get my fill of TV.

"I don't rightly think it odd, Your Majesty. I would miss so much if I were asked to go outside the realm, to live in the outer world. I suppose I'd want a bit of home with me, too." She vanished into the attached closet. "What about your spring blue corset and the navy skirt?"

Druise was forever trying to steer me toward skirts. I knew that Strict had put her up to it, trying to encourage me to dress more the part, and some days I deliberately refused just to annoy him. But today, I refused because I wasn't sure when I'd be called out. A lot rode on the shoulders of what the men found at both the Wilding Fae village and the site where *The Wave Catcher* had sunk. Speaking of…

"Have people been discussing the ship?" I called to her. "I'll take my blue corset and a pair of jeans. Boots, not heels or slippers."

After a moment, Druise reappeared, clothing in hand. "Yes, Your Majesty. There is little else being spoken of."

"And what are they saying?" I was hoping not to hear what she said next, but I wasn't surprised.

"That perhaps Myst is back, her spirit returned. That perhaps…the Vampiric Fae have a hand in the disappearance of the crew. There is much fear, Your Majesty, and very little trust that we will find out before whatever it is comes for the Barrow."

And there it was. They still didn't trust me. Their Barrow had been taken from them once, and they feared it would happen again. While I had led the fight against Myst, and we had killed her, they didn't trust me to rule them and keep them safe. I was an outsider. Every day, in some way, I was reminded of that one fact. And every day, I tried to make inroads on it—to do something to bring the people closer to me.

Some were welcoming, but others were openly hostile. Oh, no one was deliberately rude to my face—Check would gut them for it, and he was always by my side when I was out and about. But the looks…the whispers…I knew what people were saying. And I also knew that barring assassination, they had little choice but to grudgingly accept me.

"I know they don't trust me, Druise. But it still hurts when I hear it." I sighed. There wasn't much I could do about it, either. They were stuck with me, and I was stuck with them. I couldn't abdicate. If I did, I'd start to age immediately and have to journey to the Golden Isle. And I just wasn't ready for that.

"Oh please, Your Majesty—I didn't mean it like that." The look on her face made me jump to reassure her.

"I know, Druise. I know you didn't mean it—please, don't worry." I had learned the hard way that Druise had an extremely soft heart, and she also had a deep sense of responsibility, which meant she often assumed guilt that wasn't hers to assume.

I let her lace me into the corset after I slid on my jeans. She brushed my hair and fixed on my crown as I put on my makeup. Grieve was still asleep, but given we always had to appear at breakfast together, I motioned to Druise.

"I'm ready now. You can go. Thank you." I never forgot to say thanks, given how roughly I knew some of the nobles treated their servants. That was next on my agenda —creating a special set of rules for how servants and workers were treated, though I knew that would go over like a lead balloon and there would be a lot of backlash. The Fae were not the most congenial of people to begin with, and the Winter Fae? Even less so.

She curtseyed, then quietly withdrew from the room. As she closed the door behind her, I leaned over Grieve and kissed his cheek. "Wake up, sleepyhead. We have to get down to breakfast and check on how things went at the village of the Wilding Fae."

He blinked, then flashed me a lazy smile and held out his arms. "Why don't we take a break first?"

"As tempting as that is, I don't think we have the leeway this morning. Not with the way the news about *The Wave Chaser* has gone over."

As he pushed back the covers and slid out of bed, I told him what Druise had said about the rumors going around. "We have to quash the idea that Myst is back. I don't want wholesale panic."

Grieve stretched, his naked body an invitation to run my tongue along his chest...and other places. But I restrained myself. "But...is it?" he asked.

I stared at him. "What do you mean?"

"I mean, is it a rumor? Could there be any truth to the idea? I think that before we go blowing smoke away, we'd better make sure there isn't truly a fire to worry about in the first place." The look on his face terrified me. He was actually considering the chance that Myst might have returned.

As he dressed—the clothing that appeared were his royal togs, which told me he was taking this seriously—I wandered over to the mirror and stared at my reflection. Myst, the Queen of the Indigo Court, had been my mother in a different life. My soul still bore energy from the Vampiric Fae. Grieve and I had been on opposite sides in that lifetime, but we had still met and fallen in love, and we had died for our love. The thought that the cruel queen might have returned stabbed my stomach like the tip of a sharp dagger.

"I can't believe that she might be back. I can't let myself believe it. I destroyed her heartstone. I killed her. She has to be gone because I don't know if I could take her on again." My voice was barely a whisper.

Grieve took me by the shoulders, pressing against my back as he nuzzled my neck, then turned me around for a full-on kiss, deep and passionate and darkly reassuring.

"I *don't* think she's back, but we must make certain. We have to look into all possibilities. What happened to the hundreds of people aboard *The Wave Chaser*—we can't let any stone go unturned in our investigation. So, we will look into the chance that Myst has returned, or that someone among the remnants of her people has taken up the banner. We won't assume it so, but we will check it out to eliminate the possibility."

His voice was no-nonsense, and his practicality cut through the haze of fear that had risen. He stroked my cheek as I took a deep breath.

"Thank you," I whispered.

"For what?"

"For being you. Come on, let's get down to breakfast." I took his hand and we headed out of the room. Check was waiting outside—he slept in shifts and was always with me when I went about the Barrow in public, but today instead of Fearless, he was with a guard whose name was Truce.

"Fearless requested a personal day. His mother is ill

and he wanted to go see her. She lives in a village far out on one of the floes—Shinetown." Check jerked his head toward Truce. "So Truce will be taking over for today if that's all right with you, Your Majesty."

"That's fine." Technically, he should have checked with me first, but Check knew that I was lenient, especially given family matters, and I had the feeling that when he said Fearless's mother was *ill*, he meant *gravely ill*. Otherwise, he would have okayed it with me before letting the guard take time.

We headed toward the dining hall. "Check, Druise said the mood following the announcement of the ship sinking was restless and that rumors are going around about Myst?"

Check cleared his throat. "She's correct. Unfortunately, people will talk and there's not much we can do to stop it until you make some sort of official proclamation regarding the validity of the speculation." He paused. "Your Majesty, I'm worried…"

His pause froze me in my tracks. "You don't think she's back, do you?" I kept my voice low. Grieve paused by my side, and Truce stood back, his jaw set as if he were deliberately keeping his ears to himself.

"No, I don't, but there's something out there. The guards returned from Whitecroft—the village of the Wilding Fae. Begging your pardon, Your Majesty, but we're shit out of luck, as you would say. What they found was brutal and terrifying."

"Why didn't you wake us when they returned?"

"Because I knew you'd be up soon—they've only just returned this past hour."

I glanced at Grieve, then back at Check. "Order breakfast to be brought to us in our council room. Send for Strict, and for Captain Shell. Also, I may need to visit Thorn, to see what he has to say. On the chance, prepare for a trip into the shamans' lair."

❋

ONCE STRICT AND SHELL—CAPTAIN of the Guard—arrived in the council chamber, we settled in around the table. Check was there, and Truce. We also asked Shell to bring Warring and Hezemie—his lieutenants. They worked directly beside him and were his right-hand men. Check would have had Shell's job if he hadn't been assigned as my personal guard. I'd asked him once if being passed over had bothered him. His only answer was, "Whatever pleases you most, Your Majesty, pleases me."

After the food had been brought in, and the servants dismissed, Truce took his place outside the door. Check guarded the inside.

I spread butter and jam on fresh, hot bread and relaxed as the yeasty warmth exploded in my mouth. Even my taste buds had changed since I had undergone my initiation—food tasted stronger, more vibrant to me, and my hunger for meats and breads and fruits and cheese had strengthened, while my desire for all the junk I used to love had—not vanished, but lessened.

"So, tell us. What did they find?"

"About a mile outside of Whitecroft, there's a stone ring the Wilding Fae use for ritual. A couple of the Fae were out there when something attacked them. Your Majesty, the attack was brutal. Whoever perpetrated it wasn't focused on simply killing them, but on ripping them to shreds. I can see why rumors might be circulating that the Indigo Court has risen again… This does remind me of the Vampiric Fae's attacks. But there was something else, something we never saw with Myst's followers. There were scorch marks—ice burns."

"Ice burns?" I wasn't familiar with the term.

"Ice magic. The Elementals can cause ice burns, but they won't, not unless they are provoked. These were on the trees, on the snow, on the remnants of the bodies that were left. Something blasted through there, something that either has an innate ability, or the knowledge of how to use the magic of ice. We questioned the Wilding Fae as best as we could. There were sightings of a fierce, large shadow of a wolf. This wolf stood as tall as man, and was a smoky black with glowing blue eyes."

I frowned, sitting back. "That sounds *nothing* like what Myst had up her sleeve. Ice spiders, yes, though those abound through the realm on their own. She just harnessed them into her service. But a shadow of a wolf? Where did they see it?"

"On the outskirts of Whitecroft, at evensong. Never a clear view, but several sightings over the past few days."

As we paused to eat—I was famished and Grieve was hungry, too—I thought over what they had said. Finally, after finishing my steak and eggs, I pushed away my plate.

"Could it be some strange Cambyra Fae? A wolf-shifter gone mad?" Truth was, not every member of the Fae race could be trusted. In fact, the ones who went bad, usually went very, very bad and caused far more damage than the average human sociopath.

Captain Shell shook his head. "Your Majesty perhaps forgets the nature of the Wilding Fae. For some creature to not only surprise *two* of them, but actually manage to kill *both* without being heard and stopped…"

"Good point." Most of the Wilding Fae were strong enough to take on every person in this room. And most of the Wilding Fae would come out victorious. Two of them? Should have been able to handle any ordinary attacker.

"What about the Wilding Fae themselves? Anyone reporting a troublemaker in Whitecroft? Did anyone say anything that might point to this being one of their own?"

Again, Shell shot me down. "No, and you can be certain that if they thought it an internal incident, the killer would have been dispatched without coming to the Barrow. The Wilding Fae take care of their own. That they sought out Your Majesty's help shows they're frightened."

"He's right." Strict shrugged. He had picked up the gesture from me. "The Wilding Fae fear very little, and they have no patience for anyone who disrupts the flow of their world. They couldn't take on Myst and her entire army, so they worked with us. That they petitioned the Crown for help tells us they fear this is a problem beyond their scope to handle."

"Not a good sign, then." My heart sank. I didn't want to deal with a sociopathic wolf, but it looked like we had one on our hands.

At that moment, there was a tap at the door. Check opened it while we fell silent. A whisper or two later, he quietly closed the door.

"Your Majesty, I do not wish to interrupt you, but Truce says that one of our men has news of *The Wave Catcher*. Shall I escort him in?"

I rubbed my head. Everything always seemed to happen at once. "Please do."

Check opened the door and a young guardsman entered. I recognized his face, but couldn't quite place his name. He dropped to one knee, then slowly rose and stood at attention.

"You have news for us?" I motioned for him to take a step closer. Check shadowed him to make certain that he behaved himself.

"Yes, Your Majesty. *The Wave Catcher*...I don't know how to tell you this, but the ship is back on the water, sort of."

"What do you mean? It sank." The day was just getting better and better.

"That's the thing. We know it sank, but I'm telling you —we can see it sitting next to the dock. The hole is in its side, and the whole galleon looks...misty. Translucent. Not only that, but the crew and passengers seem to be there. They are disembarking...then they walk up the snow field a ways and vanish. We can see through them, too. They're spirits, Your Majesty."

I stared at him, unable to comprehend what the hell was happening. "You saw the ship rise?"

"Yes, we were there. The ship rose out of the water as a great howling—like that of a hundred wolves—filled the air."

Ghosts? We had a ghost ship full of spirits on our hands? I motioned for him to leave.

"Say nothing about this. Wait in the hall with Truce. If you're hungry, ask for a tray." After he left, I turned to the others. "Apparently the ship wasn't happy staying beneath the waves. Let's go. We need to find out what's going on."

✸

CAPTAIN SHELL, his lieutenants, five of the elite guard,
Check, and Truce accompanied us as Grieve and I led the
journey, setting out for the shore of the Crashing Sea.

As we hurried along, racing over the snows, I flashed
back to before my initiation, before my body had changed
as the heartstone emerged from me. I had been weaker
then, and much more vulnerable, but one thing this stint
had taught me: *nobody* was immortal, without chance of
dying. And as the saying went: no one here gets out alive.
While I felt myself still transforming, changes came
slowly, and probably with good reason. Become a
different person in the blink of an eye and it's easy to lose
the person you were. Slowly shift, and you keep the best
of both worlds. At least, that was how I hoped it would
play out in the end.

We hurried through the forests. The trees here
towered into the sky, dark conifers that could survive in
the realm of Winter. They were brooding, and alive, and
while I had yet to hear them speak, at times I felt them
watching me—as if they were contemplating my place in
their world. As we passed a clearing, a group of Ice
Elementals wandered by, slowing as I drew near. They
were bipedal, shaped like very tall humans formed of
bluish-clear ice. No features marred their faces. Their
arms and legs were angular, like icicles. As soon as I
stepped forward, the pack stopped. There were five of
them, and they turned toward me, pausing.

They are unbound, Cicely. You should tie them to you.
Ulean's gentle voice tickled at my ear.

They are unaligned? Very well.

I closed my eyes, raising my hand as I let myself slip into the slipstream. As the astral wind buffeted me, I reached out to them. *I am your queen. Guard this place and bind yourselves to my service. Should anyone counter to my will enter this area, destroy them.*

A moment later I felt the connection take and hold. It was as if I had reached off of a web—held out my hand and offered them the chance to join my world. A moment passed, then another, and finally, one by one they moved onto my path, into my journey, binding themselves to my power. I opened my eyes. The Elementals gazed at me, unspeaking, but then nodded and spread out, moving at a steady pace, sparkling under the sky that forever shadowed the realm of Snow and Ice. They would keep to their task until I gave them permission to stop, or until some spell countered my will.

They all love you, Cicely. Or...as close to love as they can get. There is no name, truly, for how the Elementals look at you. You are the core of their essence, now. You are their world.

I let out my breath and turned to the others. "They now belong to us. They will watch this area." A petal-soft kiss touched my face and I glanced up. The sky was clouding over and a light scattering of snow had started. "Come. We haven't far to go."

We threaded our way through the forest and then veered off to the left onto a broad path of compacted snow. It had been traversed so many times it would never melt, a solid sheet of chunky ice. The new snow that fell on top of it usually drifted to the sides in the wind. Some of the snow banks would melt. There *were* seasons here in the realm of Snow and Ice, but spring and summer were just warmer winters, and the temperature never rose above the low thirties. Sometimes just high enough for the top layers of snow to trickle away and freeze later.

As we came out of the forest I breathed a sigh of relief. The path wasn't long, but it could be dangerous if you met the Winter Wolves along the way, or snow spiders or the giant ice serpents that hid in the mountains and rock formations that dotted the vast snow fields.

Not fifty yards from the edge of the forest was the edge of the Crashing Sea, foaming and churning as it sloshed against the edge of the ice sheet. I hadn't yet figured out if we were on a gigantic glacier or what, but I had learned that once in the realm of Fae, it was best not to ask too many questions. The answers were usually difficult to comprehend and just gave me a headache.

As we slowed, staring at the waves, I caught my breath. There, resting on the water, bobbing as the currents rolled beneath it, was the ghostly shape of *The Wave Catcher*.

Ulean shifted, her gusts brushing my face. *Something is wrong, Cicely—something is terribly wrong here.*

It was as though the galleon was formed of mist— smoke encapsulated within a pale framework. We could see through to the lower levels, all with the same translucent shimmer. The hole in the hull gaped, raw and wounded, and the masts were battered, the sails tattered and torn. But more startling than the ship was the trail of passengers that disembarked along a ghostly plank leading to the shore. They looked neither right nor left, simply marched slowly off the ship.

I moved forward, stepping into the path of the oncoming traffic. The man coming toward me didn't even blink. Instead, he passed through me, unflinching, and a bone-deep chill hit me to the core. Cold beyond the cold of the realm. Cold as *deep in the grave* cold. Cold as in *depths of the ocean* cold. And they kept coming.

Cicely, move. Do not let them touch you—even though it seems they are shades or memories of what might be, there is far more to it than that. Move, please. Ulean was frantic now, and I tried to step out of the way, but my feet wouldn't obey. I stood there, letting them pass through me until Check yanked me to one side.

"Pardon me, Your Majesty, but you don't know if any of them are dangerous."

Shaken out of my startlement, I nodded. "Of course, you're right." But I couldn't take my eyes off of the parade of the dead. And then, perhaps ten minutes, perhaps half an hour later, I noticed the same man who had first passed through me. He was walking off the ship again, and as I looked closely, I recognized several of the other faces. Men, women, children, they kept coming and coming but in a circular pattern.

I pointed it out to the others and we waited, watching closely. Sure enough, over and over the dead passed by, and when the last marched past us, the man whom I had first encountered was there again, followed by the rest.

"They're caught in a loop. But why did they return? And where are the bodies? They weren't aboard the ship." I had no clue how to deal with spirits or ghost ships. Nothing I had ever done prepared me for this.

Grieve moved forward, gazing at the parade of the dead. "There's something about them…I don't even know if they are spirits. I don't have any sense of…being-ness. Is this a picture show?" He reached out for my hand. "I'm as confused as you are, love."

Are they ghosts, Ulean?

Not ghosts, no. But I don't know...they are unnatural—they should not be. Their presence signifies something has gone terribly awry.

"Your Majesty—look at the water surrounding the ship." Check headed over to the edge of the floe and pointed toward the rippling waves sloshing beneath *The Wave Catcher.*

At first I wasn't sure what he was addressing before I realized that the waves were indeed crashing *beneath* the ship. As though there was weight bearing down on them. But if the ship was merely an image—or even a ghostly remnant—they should be frothing as normal. Check stood there, staring into the water, as puzzled as I was.

"What's going on here, guys?" I backed away. The endless circle of spirits—or whatever they were—was starting to make me dizzy. I thought I heard Ulean calling to me, but couldn't focus on her voice and the next moment, a drive so strong I couldn't ignore it hit me and I backed away, instantly transforming into my owl self.

I took wing, panicked beyond reason, unable to get my bearings. I headed out over the water, not knowing where I was going. The next moment, a great horned owl swooped in beside me. I realized it was Hunter, my grandfather. In the flurry of chaos, he was trying to guide me away from the open water back to the shore. As I tried to steady myself, he circled wide and I followed his cue. We were past the water, then back over land. As Hunter came in for a landing, I followed suit and transformed back into my normal shape as we landed on branches that were scattered with patches of snow.

I turned to my grandfather. "Where did you come from?" He hadn't come with us.

"I was in the woods as you passed. As I watched the water under that ship, I realized that it's not what it seems." He slid his arm around me and we headed back to the others, who were running up.

Cicely, you almost flew out into the open ocean. You would have...there is some sort of portal near here. Some sort of vortex. I can feel it calling to me. I must take wind and return to the Barrow so it doesn't overpower my will.

And like that, Ulean swept away, back toward our home.

Check was pale—looking terrified. He skidded to a halt, dropping to one knee in front of me. "Your Majesty, forgive me. Please, forgive me. I wasn't there to protect you."

I knew that he would fall on his sword for me if need be. And that was his job, but this was something nobody could have anticipated.

"Stand up and leave it be. None of us expected this. Hell, we don't even know what *this* is. Ulean says there's some sort of a portal near here. A vortex that lures people in. Until we know what we're dealing with, let's get the hell out of here."

Even as I spoke, a great howling rose on the wind. Loud and mournful, the call of a wolf who sounded the size of a mountain ricocheted through the air. The sound of terror, the sound of hunger, and the sound of a creature out on the hunt.

I gasped, looking around, trying to figure out where it was coming from. Immediately, the guards surrounded

Grieve and me as Hunter took to the sky, soaring up above us.

My heart was racing. "What the hell is that?"

"I don't know," Grieve whispered. "I have never heard such a keening in my life."

But in my heart, I knew it was the sound of death come to call, of the hunter spying his prey. We were on the menu of whatever this creature was and the only thing I could think about was to get away from the noise and the fear. The chaos in my mind continued, and I realized that I was so caught in the panic that it had to have a magical component.

"The sound—cover your ears. It sets off a fear reaction." Holding my hands to my ears, I headed back toward the woods. "We need to get out of the area, now. We don't have the resources to fight whatever is coming our way. Not with us, not today."

The guards formed a circle around us as we headed back into the forest. The trees felt ominous now, hiding dangers rather than guardian sentinels, and all I could think about was the need to get away from here—the need to get back to the Barrow.

All along the way, the horrible howling continued and it stopped only when we passed through the doors of the Barrow. Check waited a moment, then stepped outside again. When he returned he shook his head.

"It's still sounding in the night. I can't imagine what the villages must be thinking. We must send men to them, to let them know we are aware of the danger. We can't ignore them and expect them not to show up here, panicked."

Ulean was waiting for us. *Cicely, I would not have run if*

I had not feared I might be turned beyond my will. I apologize for leaving you there.

No, you did what you had to in order to take care of yourself. Never apologize for that, Ulean. But whatever it is, there is danger, and we must find out what we are facing.

I turned back to Check. "Then do what we must. Contact Strict and tell him to meet us in the council chamber. And I think…Grieve and I must pay a journey to the shamans. We have to speak with Thorn." As I hurried into our bedroom, Druise was there, waiting. "Prepare one of my dresses. I will attend Court, and then the shamans. I must dress the part of the Queen today, Druise. Cold and brilliant and collected."

"As you will, Your Majesty." And then she went to work, transforming me into the Queen of Snow and Ice, whose people would trust her unconditionally.

CHAPTER FOUR

B y the time I headed into the throne room, I was wearing a silver dress that shimmered with crystal beads. It had a sweetheart corset top, and a flowing skirt that barely touched the ground. It was wearable out in the snow as well as when I held court, and the material was warm. It was a synthetic, actually, though no one in my Barrow would ever know that except for Grieve and Druise. I had balked at heavy weaves that would weigh me down and insisted that the seamstresses who made my garments accept the fact that I was coming in from the outside—I wasn't fully Cambyra Fae and I had lived in the outer world for most of my life. They reluctantly agreed, after Strict intervened for me.

Druise had brought out a cloak—jet black, trimmed with crystal beading. She made sure my makeup was heavy handed—wide raven wings on my eyes, a deep blackberry lipstick. By the time we were done, I looked a little older, a lot more elegant, and most important— imposing as hell. I slid into the black ankle boots she held for me. They had stiletto heels, which I hated, but right now, it was vital that I look the part, given the circumstances. I could walk well enough in them, but I sure as hell wouldn't go on a jaunt into the woods wearing them.

Grieve dressed as well, in a jet-black tunic coat, with gray trousers. His shock of platinum hair stood out in stark contrast to the black of the coat. As he held out his arm and I laid my hand on his forearm, the surreal feel of it washed over me.

We followed the guards into the throne room. People were packed in and lined both sides of the brilliant royal blue carpet leading up to our thrones, and they curtseyed and bowed as we passed. The palace chamber was magical and dark. The dome over our thrones was inlaid with sapphire and opal, with moonstone and iolite and lapis lazuli, and our thrones themselves were carved from two ancient yew trees, adorned with silver and crystal.

We paused for a beat, turning in unison once we had ascended the stairs to the thrones, and then at the same time, we settled ourselves. A trumpeter announced that Court was officially open and we were ready for business. Strict was standing to my right. I looked up at him, and—as the crowds quieted down—nodded.

He solemnly stepped forward, standing a few steps down so that his head was lower than ours, and unfurled a long scroll. I had tried to talk them into using flat paper for decrees—standard copy paper size—but so far they had resisted my arguments that it made them easier to file, sticking to the rolling scrolls. I was determined, though, to have my way eventually.

"Her Majesty Cicely, Queen of the Court of Snow and Ice, and His Majesty Grieve, King of the Court of Snow and Ice, convene the court, this seventh day of the Moon, Year One—PM, Year 204 of the Twenty-fifth Cycle of the Lunar Owl."

PM. Post-Myst. We had decided there had to be an addendum to the yearly cycle that the Courts used, given Myst had caused such chaos and torn apart the Fae courts so dreadfully. We could never forget her—and to my mind, we *should never* forget such an enemy who had been able to bring down both Summer and Winter Courts. History had a tendency to repeat mistakes that were swept under the rug.

After a beat, Strict once again spoke. "Her Majesty, Queen of the Court of Snow and Ice, will be speaking to you briefly but she will not accept questions at this time."

I waited for him to move to the side, then stood. I had thought about what to say—and half-thought we should wait until Grieve and I visited the shamans, but Strict had convinced me that wasn't the best idea. I needed to at least address the subject.

I took a deep breath. "My people, welcome and well-met. I will dispense with niceties and come to the point. You have heard about the tragedy of *The Wave Catcher*, and perhaps you have heard of the killings out in White-croft, the village of the Wilding Fae. Today, there was another mystery—the horrible keening of the wolf that was heard throughout the floes. I will be honest—we don't yet know what we're facing, but His Majesty and I will be consulting with the shamans and we hope to have answers soon. Rest assured, whatever we are facing, we will face it together, with strength, and courage, and might. The Court of Snow and Ice is strong. We defeated one of the most deadly despots in history. The fact that we were able to conquer Myst, the Queen of the Indigo Court, signifies that we can face—and overcome—any other challenge that might come to our land."

I paused, trying to assess the feel of the room.

Ulean, what do you think? What's the reaction?

They want answers, but the energy...there are whispers in the slipstream, Cicely. I think you have some leeway here, but you are Queen. They will expect some answers soon. After Myst, there is still so very much fear.

Understood.

I took a deep breath, then—rather than add anything that might dilute my message, I said, "Go about your day. Don't walk through the woods unescorted. Look after your neighbors, if you live outside the Barrow. The best way to stay safe is to stand together. We will update you as soon as we can on this situation."

And then, I backed up the steps. Lainule had taught me: Never turn your back on a crowd unless you are leaving a room. As I stood in front of my throne, Grieve rose to his feet. Surrounded by guards, we headed out through the door behind the raised daïs that was reserved for our use only. Strict followed. The remaining guards would make sure that the spectators left the hall peacefully.

Once we were back in the council chamber, a servant was waiting with a basket of food. I had learned my lesson. Journeying to the shamans required far more than just taking a stroll into another section of the Barrow and last time, I had been so hungry I almost passed out. Think realm within another realm. Deep within the Court of Snow and Ice, the shamans were walled off by an even greater divide.

One thing I had learned quickly when I took over the crown and moved into the Barrow was that reality was mutable, and that in this world nothing remained fixed. In fact, the words *this world* were a misnomer. There were worlds within worlds all over the planet. Layers of existence overlapped—hell, in some places they coexisted—just in different planes. One step to the left or right could shift one's surroundings by a quantum leap. It had crossed my mind that—if we were able to see every plane of existence at once—we'd go mad from all the conflicting visuals. It would be as if Escher had taken a paintbrush to the world.

And so, eating our sandwiches and pastries as we walked, we began the journey into the depths of the Barrow. No one was allowed into these parts of the Court without being royalty, upper-tier guard, or personally summoned by the shamans. We were headed to a center of the Court—its very heart and soul, kept and watched over by the shamans.

The shamans made life in this realm possible. Even the Winter Fae would not be able to exist here without the shamans dreaming it into a place where life could flourish. Without their magic, the cold would freeze every drop of blood in the body and the wanderer would stand as a statue, forever encased in the snow and ice.

The tunnel leading to their abode twisted and turned, soon morphing into a tunnel of ice that stretched out from the edge of the Barrow, traversing beneath the ice fields that made up our lands. The walls and floor of the passage shimmered with sparks of light—soft white and gentle violet. The first time I had journeyed to the shamans, I thought I might be walking forever, the passage going on and on, seemingly endless.

We quieted down as the air grew thick and chill. Noise seemed to shatter it, echoing on for miles. Even Ulean remained silent, although I knew she was with me. As we journeyed along through the corridor, I sank into my thoughts.

This is my life. This is what it will be for centuries to come.

The thought sprung into my mind, stark and terrifying. Yet, somehow, it also comforted me. So many people didn't know what they were meant to do. The vast majority lived their lives in a blur—trudging through their days, hating their jobs, wasting time without really thinking about how short life could be. There was an advantage to living consciously. No matter what one's life span was, the ability to make a choice about how we spent our time…that was a great gift, and one that only we could give to ourselves. Even if it was only an hour a day, claiming control over what we did with that hour—it made a difference.

Check turned around. "We're near the barrier, Your Majesty."

I blinked and looked around. The color of the ice had shifted from blue to purple. Purple was the color of the shamans' magic.

Peering around him, I could see a gauzy veil of energy completely shrouding the end of the corridor. As we entered the cloud of energy, a mass of sparks sizzled, darting across my body. The last time I had ventured here, I had closed my eyes out of fear. Now, I knew what to expect. But the jolts of energy were still disrupting.

If we had been enemies? Those jolts would have been

deadly.

We passed through the veil into a chamber completely formed of ice. Even the furniture was carved from chunks of the glistening frozen water. Shadows moved along the walls—the shamans were watching us. Even within this altered dimension, they lived still another step out. As we took our place around a circular table, a shadow began to emerge from the ice.

Thorn, the Speaker for the council of shamans.

He was a short man, wearing leather pants and a fur cloak. His chest—muscled and gleaming—was bare, and his long dark hair was braided with beads and feathers.

"Your Majesty, you grace us with your presence." The words were proper, but the energy behind them was matter-of-fact. The shamans did not engage in chitchat.

"We have questions. There are two situations we are facing, and I have no idea what to make of them." I leaned toward him. "We need your counsel."

Thorn pulled out a bag from his pocket. He held my gaze and it felt as though he was looking right through me, deep into my core. The shamans were Fae, I knew that much, but just what kind, I had no clue.

"You seek advice about a ship and about two deaths. Two seemingly disparate problems, but at the core—the threads of both issues lead to one answer. They are not disconnected." He opened the bag and tossed what looked like bone chips on the table. "Pick five."

I stared at the chips, wondering what animal they were from. *Or person?*

"The second," he said, reading my thoughts. "They are bone chips from Speakers past. And when I die, my bones will join theirs."

I decided it was better not to ask anything else about them. The shamans were frightening enough without knowing all of their secrets. I sucked in a deep breath and chose five of the bone fragments and handed them to him.

He laid them out, one by one. Then he picked up the first and clenched it in his fist. A moment later, he added the second, then the third—fourth, and fifth. After he was done, he lowered his head, eyes closed.

The energy in the room grew thick. My body felt heavy, and I wanted to sleep. I closed my eyes, sliding back in my chair.

✳

I WAS STANDING on board a ship, on the deck, and the waves of the sea were growing choppy.

The ship was huge, filled with families. As I watched, they rushed this way and that—trying to tighten down anything that threatened to slide around. A great storm had risen in back of the ship, and was bearing down on us quickly. Clouds, gray and pendulous, roiled through the sky, churning as the storm overtook the ship. Crew members raced around, shouting orders to get below before the deluge hit.

I caught my breath, watching as people scattered, struggling to get to the stairwells that led below decks. The waves swelled, rising up to splash across the boat. I cringed as a wall of water came toward me, but as it passed through me as though I didn't exist, I realized that I was only seeing what had happened. I wasn't actually there.

That gave me the courage to straighten up and look around.

The storm was really bearing down now, engulfing the boat with cloud and wind. And then, the snow began to fall. Not scattered flakes, but a harsh flurry that verged on a whiteout.

As the mayhem on deck increased, I had a sudden feeling that something was watching from the stern of the ship. I turned, slowly making my way toward the rear of the boat. The screams grew louder as the boat shifted, listing dangerously to the starboard side. For me, moving presented no problem—but the people who were actually aboard were slipping and falling as the waves swelled, tossing the boat around.

And then, I was at the back end, staring into a great wall of water that rose behind the ship. *Tidal wave? Tsunami?* My first thought was that it was going to sweep down and wash everyone off the deck, and my heart caught in my throat.

But then, I saw something. *A man's face in the wave, staring directly at me.*

His features were harsh and angular, his eyes ruthless. Then, a cunning grin, and he whispered something. I could hear the voice on the edge of the slipstream but couldn't make out the words. The next thing I knew, a wall of frost rolled toward the boat like a wave of water. As it passed over the stern, I braced myself.

Like the water and wind, it passed through me. But as it passed over the crew and passengers, they froze into place, then shattered into white plumes of frost. They vanished, as though they had never existed.

I caught sight of Sweet Pea. Her eyes wide with fear,

she turned to race below. The frost passed over her, but it was as though a barrier—a force field—kept it from touching her. She vanished into the hold.

The face in the wave began to laugh, then opened his mouth and sucked all of the wisps of frost that had once been the crew and passengers into his mouth. He swallowed them, and then—

—I was back.

※

I OPENED MY EYES, breathing hard. My heart was racing and I leaned forward, elbows on the table, trembling and relieved to be out of the vision. The experience had been too visceral, entirely too real. But the flush of relief passed, replaced by horror.

I began to shiver, wrapping my cloak tightly around my shoulders. "He took them. He turned them to frost and then snorted them up like a crack head. He fed on their life essences, didn't he?" I gazed at Thorn.

"Yes, Cicely. He did just that."

"Who is he and what does he want? And how is he connected to Whitecroft?"

Thorn pressed his lips together, then let out a faint sigh. "He is Fenrick, the harbinger of the Jötnar—the frost giants from the realm of Jötunheim."

I shifted. "Not *Fenrir*? You can't be talking about the Fenris wolf?" Thoughts of the great shadowy wolf figure the Wilding Fae had seen crossed my mind and I edged one step closer to panic.

"No, not Fenrir. Fenrick was a priest of Hel until she cast him out because he was too power-hungry. He took up with the frost giants, and while I do not know his full tale, I do know that Fenrick is looking to help them find their way into the realm of Snow and Ice. Presumably to be one step closer to the outer world—which they call Midgard. But he brings with him his faithful hounds—the *vargr*—evil wolves known as *wargs* in your tongue."

I rested my elbows on the table, cupping my chin. This was worse than I imagined it. "What was I seeing? What exactly did he do with the people on *The Wave Catcher*?"

"As you surmised, he froze them and fed off their life force. He is a powerful magician and a terrifying foe. I do not believe we can fight him at this point. At best, I think you might be able to drive him out of the realm, but I doubt you can kill him," Thorn said, blunt and to the point.

I shook my head. "How do we do that? And why is he attacking now?"

"Word must have traveled through the World Tree that a new Fae Queen has taken over the realm of Snow and Ice. A queen who has not yet come into her full power. As the years go by, your magic will strengthen and others will fear you—they will think twice about attacking the realm. But make no mistake, Your Majesty, the throne is still vulnerable. *You* are vulnerable."

Another thought struck me. "If I'm vulnerable to the frost giants, won't that mean the fire giants might be eyeing Rhiannon as a target? Send word to their shamans at once, Thorn. I want them on alert."

"As you wish." He paused. "In the old days, Summer and Winter would never have helped each other. They were at odds."

"In the not-so-old days, division caused both realms to fall to Myst."

"This is a new day."

"I am a new queen—and so is my cousin. The old ways are gone. You know what isolationism did. Myst was able to drive her forces into both Summer and Winter and she almost won. Another enemy could do the same. *Fenrick* could do the same. I don't plan on allowing anything of the sort to happen." I frowned, tapping my fingers on the icy table. "All right, we know who we're facing. So tell me, how did he get here? And how do we drive him out? And what about the wargs? Can we fight them? Kill them? Or are they as invulnerable as Fenrick?"

"So many questions. One answer at a time. Fenrick is not invulnerable, but he is too powerful for you to fight. *Yet.* There may come a day when you can take him on."

I nodded. "Then, how did he get here?"

"That is easier. He had to have opened a gateway from Jötunheim. Therefore, it should still be open and active. My guess is that he's scouting before the Jötnar decide to take action."

"Then we have to find the gateway and push him back through, I guess. What about the vargr? Tell us about them." It sounded easier than it was going to be—that much I knew for a fact. But still…at least we weren't facing Myst again.

Thorn held up his hand, pointing at the ice wall behind him. An image appeared—that of a giant wolf, with inky black fur and ice-white eyes. He was huge—he looked shoulder high to me.

My wolf tattoo shifted, almost whimpered, and I reached out to take Grieve's hand. He, too, was afraid. It occurred to me that anybody who *wasn't* afraid of a creature like this would be a fool. Grieve gave my fingers a long squeeze as I took a deep breath, held it a moment, then slowly released it as I tried to relax.

"The vargr are more than standard wolves. Wolves, in general, are beautiful animals. They have neither good nor evil natures, and they respond as most creatures do, depending on how they are treated. They hunt when hungry, they have a tight pack structure. But the vargr have an intelligence that rivals that of yummanii or Fae. They don't think like we do, but they are cunning and capable of solving problems and laying traps. Their blood lust is strong, and they delight in tearing their victims to pieces."

"Like they did the Wilding Fae. But how did they sneak up on them? The Wilding Fae are strong. Far stronger than the Cambyra, and they have magic of their own."

Thorn glanced at me. "The vargr can lurk in the shadows and move silently. They can also mesmerize. They can paralyze an intended victim, almost like a form of hypnosis. Therefore, never stare into their eyes."

"Other than that, do they have any forms of magical attack?" Grieve leaned in, staring at the image, a thoughtful look on his face.

"Two forms, actually. The first is a form of ice magic—they can burn with their bite. You would call it freezer burn, Cicely."

"That explains the wounds on the victims." I glanced over at Captain Shell and he nodded.

"It would be consistent with what we found, yes."

Thorn continued. "Their second magical attack is also

dangerous. They can mimic voices, and lure their victims into danger through their tricks. The most likely is for one of the vargr to call for help in a child's voice. When their intended prey comes running to the rescue, the vargr are ready to ambush. From there, it's easy for them to mesmerize their victim and then tear them to shreds. Unlike wolves, the vargr also hunt for pleasure. They enjoy the kill, and they enjoy seeing others in pain. It's rumored that the vargr are evil spirits come back in wolfen form."

Thorn stood and crossed to where the image was still plastered across the ice wall. He pointed to the area just below the wolf's throat. "This is their most vulnerable place. They have an Achilles heel. Right in this place—at the base of the throat—is a magical regulator that allows them to travel to other realms besides Jötunheim—it controls metabolism. Pierce the area with an arrow or spear or dagger, and it will short-circuit the magic. You won't kill them, but you will send them back home and they won't be able to return unless someone heals them. And healing is not likely, given the nature of the Jötnar. They tend to feed on the wounded, rather than help them."

"Oh, the frost giants are sounding better and better." I shivered. "I really don't want them over here, now. So any advice on actually *killing* the vargr?"

"The same way you kill anything—heart and brain are the best targets." Thorn snapped his fingers and the image vanished.

"If Fenrick is a disgraced priest of Hel, is there some way we can approach her for help?" Captain Shell asked.

I started to say "Not a chance in hell," but Thorn beat

me to the punch.

"I would advise against it. Approaching the goddess of Death is akin to trussing yourself on a spit for a group of hungry cannibals." Thorn arched his eyebrows—something I'd never seen him do before—and snorted. "The best way to approach the goddess of Death is to give her a wide berth and hope she doesn't notice you. She seldom strikes bargains with the living and her price would be more than you want to pay."

"So, we have to drive Fenrick back through his gateway. How do we close it off afterward? And how do we get him there in the first place. Also…what about *The Wave Catcher*? What about the spirits that we are seeing? They seem to be caught in a loop, and now we know that it was Fenrick who destroyed them." There were still so many questions and not enough answers. I was feeling terribly frustrated and powerless.

"Don't forget—how do we find this gateway? What will it look like?" Grieve folded his hands on the table. He looked as worried as I felt.

The shaman waved his hand toward the ice wall again. An image flickered into sight, an archway formed of a blue fire, with ripples of energy crossing between the arches.

"This is what the gateway will look like. We do not know its specific location, but it cannot be far. The brutal weather in our realm gets worse the farther out you go and even Fenrick could not exist too far away from the Barrow and its surrounding protection. The realm of Snow and Ice is mostly uninhabitable, with only the Ice Elementals and snow creatures able to exist in the wastelands. Your Majesty…you have never been out that far, and it would not be wise until you have ruled over this realm for centuries. It will take that long for you to fully adapt."

"I'm not sure what you mean by that. I thought I had adapted."

Thorn once again held my gaze. "Cicely," he said. "There will come a day when you are as cold and stark as the realm itself. Just as Lainule would have eventually been as brilliant as the Court of Rivers and Rushes — living within the very heart of the fire—very few of the Fae Queens ever reach that stage. And the few who did became one with the realm, forever part of its essence. Most choose to return to the Golden Isle before they ever reach that point."

It was then that I understood. If I were to stay here long enough — for millennia— I would lose myself and merge into the core of Winter. That a few of the Fae Queens had chosen this route left me both awed and humbled. I honestly didn't think I would ever have what it took to let myself get to that point. But these were thoughts for another time. Another question came to mind.

"How did Fenrick affect *The Wave Catcher* when it was out at sea?" I told him what I had seen, the face in the wave.

"Fenrick is a powerful sorcerer and he can send his spirit out far ahead of him. Call it a form of bilocation. You see now why I say you are not strong enough to defeat him?"

A little part of me—the egotistical side—wanted to protest that I had managed to defeat Myst. But truth was, we had paid dearly to bring down the Queen of the Indigo

Court. We had lost many lives in doing so. I still thought she had to be stronger than Fenrick, but then I forced myself to stop thinking along those lines. The shamans were a better judge than I was. Fenrick had strong magic —magic we didn't even know about at this point. Whatever he had practiced during his time as a priest of Hel would most likely be the magic of death and destruction. I didn't want to chance my men against such an unknown factor.

"Yes, I understand. So once we find the gate, what do we do?"

Thorn frowned. "You must lure him to it. Tempt him with bait. Then, literally—shove him through. Immediately after, destroy the runes that mark the sides of the archway. There will be three runes in particular that you must deface, preferably with fire."

Once again he waved his hand and the wall of ice cleared. Another image shimmered into view, that of three runes, glowing with a faint light. "You must destroy the runes in this particular order." He pointed to first one, then the second, and finally—the third. "If you make a mistake and destroy them in a different order, the gate will never close unless Fenrick himself chooses to destroy it."

Captain Shell tilted his head. "You said we should destroy the runes with fire. Does it matter what kind of fire? Does it have to be magical?"

"That is a good question," said Thorn. "Magical fire is best, and I would suggest you seek one of the Wilding Fae who lives in the village of Whitecroft. There are at least two who can wield the destruction you need. Consult with the Snow Hag to be sure."

"They lost two of their members to the vargr. They may be willing to help us without additional payment, but whatever they request, we will grant." Part of me wanted to stay right here. I didn't want to go back and deal with all of this. But responsibility won out. "One last question. What about the spirits on the shores of the ice floe? What can we do to ease them and send them on to their afterlife?"

The shaman rubbed his chin. "The shamans will need to perform a ritual, but until Fenrick is dispatched from this realm, it will do us—and the spirits—no good. He not only drained their life force, but that gave him a hold on them. He is keeping them bound to the ship. And since the ship is at the bottom of the Crashing Sea, the spirits will wander the edge of the ice floe until they are freed from their servitude."

"So he is keeping them bound, feeding off of them even though they are already dead. It wasn't enough that he stole their life force, but he is using their spirits to fuel his power even in death. Which is why they didn't feel like ghosts. Their energy is being drained elsewhere."

Of all the things Fenrick had done since he arrived in our realm, this angered me most. It was bad enough to kill, but to then source power through their spirits afterward? Evil.

We stood. I turned to Thorn. "Thank you. Once again you have been of great service."

He nodded. "That is our purpose. We serve the realm of Snow and Ice. We serve the Court and the Queen. If you need us further, you know we are always here."

And so we turned and left, facing a battle I dreaded fighting.

CHAPTER FIVE

O ur first order of business was to find the gate. I
sent my men out in small groups, with a warning
to keep alert. We briefed them on how to dispatch the
vargr, and told them to steer clear of Fenrick if they
should see him. Meanwhile, Grieve and I took a trip to
Whitecroft. I had never been to the village of the Wilding
Fae before, and I didn't know what to expect. But when
we got there, I was surprised by how beautiful it was.

The Wilding Fae lived in burrows, and it made me
think of *The Hobbit*, which I had read when I was fifteen.
While I had seen a number of the Wilding Fae from a
distance, the only one I was familiar with was the Snow
Hag. But they were as disparate as the colors of the
rainbow—not one looked like another. They varied in
size, they varied in colors, some looked like walking twigs
with arms and legs and a head. Still others were shaped
like humans, but they might be sporting an extra eye or an
extra limb, or they might be short and squat with no neck.
And still others were even stranger, as though all the

goblins and gremlins from legend and lore had taken a trip through Picasso's brain, emerging in reality-defying forms.

Their burrows were dug into the snow, the door the only sign that it was not a simple mound of snow. As we entered the village, I saw that the walkway was lit by balls of glowing light that hovered in the air, bouncing lightly around us. I reached out to touch one and got a surprisingly strong shock as my finger met the pale pink light.

We were soon surrounded by a train of Wilding Fae, who followed us as we proceeded through the village while I sought out the Snow Hag. And then she was there, without ceremony.

"Perhaps a Queen might seek one of the Wilding Fae in her own habitat, with a request to make."

I knew that voice. I turned to see the Snow Hag coming up behind us. She dropped in a quick curtsey and then stood. Here, in her own village, she seemed more regal and her power, more apparent. I gave her a gentle nod and smiled.

"Perhaps a Queen might indeed seek one in particular in the village of the Wilding Fae. Perhaps a Queen has a question. And perhaps one of the Wilding Fae with whom she has built a friendship might have an answer."

The Snow Hag cocked her head to the side and laughed. "A Queen has become adept at speaking with the Wilding Fae, and this might please her subjects. One of the Wilding Fae who claims friendship with a Queen might inquire what it is that the Queen seeks."

I looked around the village and then back at the Snow Hag. "A Queen might seek one of the Wilding Fae who possesses the ability to create magical fire. A Queen might seek aid in destroying a magical gateway through which a deadly killer has emerged."

"One of the Wilding Fae might inquire whether this killer has attacked any in the village of Whitecroft."

"The answer to such a question would be yes. Or perhaps, the killer's servants are to blame."

The Snow Hag fell silent for a moment, closing her eyes.

I waited patiently. It never served to rush the Wilding Fae. They moved as they would—fast or slow—and no force in the world would change their pace. I got the distinct feeling that the Snow Hag was communicating with the others. There was a crackle in the air—a whisper on the slipstream that I couldn't quite catch. I wasn't sure how much time passed, but as we stood there waiting, the snow fell silently around us, dusting the ground and filling our footprints.

Finally, she opened her eyes. "One of the Wilding Fae might introduce a Queen to the one she seeks."

She turned and began walking through the village unhampered by the snow flurry, or the drifts around her. We followed. The flakes fluttered down to kiss my hair, my shoulders, my eyelashes. The snowfall muted the sounds from the village and it felt as though we were walking inside a snow globe that was perpetually being shaken—where the flurries never stopped falling.

Eventually, we reached one of the burrows on the outside of the village. The Snow Hag knocked on the door and we took our places behind her. Regardless of whether I was the Queen, the Wilding Fae were stronger than any of us. I wasn't even sure if the shamans could fight against them, should it ever come to that.

The door opened a crack. One pale green eye—as large as an orange—peered out from behind the door. The Snow Hag whispered again, and this time I caught her murmured voice on the slipstream.

Ulean, can you understand what they are saying? I can hear them talking but I do not understand the words.

They speak a dialect known solely to the Wilding Fae. I do not understand them either.

Ulean gusted around me, whirling the snowflakes into a vortex. I could create a tornado that could rip a town to shreds, I thought. But for me, it was dangerous to do so. My powers over the wind had grown incredibly strong, but my lack of control was still an issue. Until I learned how to master myself, there was always the chance that I could be taken over by the force and turn into a deadly Wind Queen, driving a tornado or gale or hurricane. Lainule had left before she could train me on how to use the fan that had given me the powers. Now, I didn't even need it to call up the winds.

A moment later, and the door opened wide. The Snow Hag motioned for us to follow her and we entered the burrow. I wasn't sure what to expect, but it looked like a tidy little home. There were several chairs, a table, and a bed in the corner. A fireplace held a roaring fire. I haven't seen any smoke emerging from the outside so I wasn't sure how it was vented, but the chamber was clear of smoke so it had to filter out somewhere.

The Wilding Fae with the large eye was standing in the corner. He had two feet and two arms, but he was short and squat, and his head was bulbous. Like a cyclops, he had only the one eye—it was beautiful, an emerald green that shimmered with magic. Below, he had a tiny nose, and a rather large mouth in the shape of an "O" that was ringed with teeth.

The Snow Hag turned to me. "This is the one whom a Queen might seek, if she seeks the power of fire. There may be a problem with language and understanding. A Wilding Fae who can breathe a magical flame may not speak the same tongue as a Queen. Perhaps there is another within this room who might be willing to translate. Would a Queen be amiss if this were to happen?"

"A Queen would appreciate a translator."

The Snow Hag turned to the Wilding Fae and began to speak. This time we all heard her, but I had no more understanding of what she was saying than I had when I heard her speaking through the slipstream. After a moment the one-eyed Wilding Fae answered back.

The Snow Hag laughed. "A Queen may call a Wilding Fae who can breathe fire the *Flammen*. And the Flammen is willing to make a deal with a Queen."

"Perhaps a translator will ask a Flammen what sort of a deal he might wish to make."

Another moment passed while she translated my request. I looked around the room. It was exceptionally tidy, as well as cozy, and had a snuggle factor that made me want to curl up in the corner and take a nap. There was something homey about this place, something welcoming about Whitecroft. I doubted most people would find it appealing, but to me it felt safe and secure, like a place you could come back to when you needed a safe haven.

She turned to me, smiling. "A deal might be struck with a Queen, and that deal would be a night of dancing and merriment in the Court chambers for the Wilding Fae."

The request surprised me. But then again, everything about the Wilding Fae surprised me. They placed value on intangible things, and seemed content with their lives. I had no idea how much wealth any of them had, or whether riches really meant anything to them. In some ways, I thought they were happier than most people I had ever met.

"Once the task is over and the journey complete, a Queen would be most honored to host a night of dancing and merriment for the Wilding Fae at her Court. If a translator would pass along this answer, a Queen would be pleased." It was a struggle to keep up the riddle-speak. But if I asked a direct question, it would be considered rude and, like as not, remain unanswered. The Wilding Fae spoke in riddles; this was their nature.

She relayed the information and within moments, we had struck a bargain. The Flammen would come to the Court and meet with my men, waiting for the moment when we found the gate. I would send a message to the Snow Hag when we set out to destroy it.

On our way home, Grieve talked to Captain Shell while I walked beside Check. The snow was falling fast and heavy now and we were in for a good blow.

"The snow never stops, does it? It just keeps on falling and piling up as the world grows up toward the sky." I wondered aloud what would happen in one hundred years. Would the Eldburry Barrow vanish beneath the weight of the snow and ice?

Check shook his head. "Remember, there is some melt

in the spring and summer here. Enough to keep the world from becoming one vast blanket of snow."

"You know, when I was fighting Myst, I couldn't wait for the winter to be over. And now here I am, Queen *of* the winter. The irony is not lost on me. And while I miss the greenery of the Golden Wood, I'm starting to feel at home here. The snow and ice are my elements now, and I think I would feel uncomfortable without them around me if it was for more than a few days. I imagine my cousin feels the same about the warmth and heat and the summer sun." And there it was—we were in transformation. Amber and jet for real. She was the sun, I was the moon. She was summer, I was winter.

"Your Majesty seems to be wandering deep in thought today. Is there something you wish for me to do?" Check was my personal bodyguard, but he was also my friend and I knew he was trying to find out if I was okay.

I smiled at him and placed a hand on his forearm as we walked along. "Everything's fine, Check. I'm just thinking about the past year. I'm sure you realize how extreme this transformation has been for me."

The guard nodded, a somber look on his face. "It cannot have been easy, Your Majesty. If you'll permit me to say, I think both you and your cousin have made remarkable gains. I do not know many people—magicborn, Fae, or yummanii—who could have made a similar transformation. You will always have my support and my loyalty, and you know I would fall on my sword for you."

"I know, and that is the greatest gift and compliment that you can give me." And then, I fell silent, wandering within the confines of my thoughts until we reached the Barrow.

❉

AT THE BARROW, Grieve and I took a break for dinner. Our men weren't back yet, so there wasn't much we could do until then. As we ate, Check tapped on our door, then peeked in.

"Your Majesty, your friend Luna, from New Forest, is here."

I stiffened. Luna and I had not parted on the best of terms. She had rashly promised her life in exchange to her ancestors for their help in destroying Myst. I blamed myself for that—but there had been no help for it. Now, she was living on borrowed time.

Since Rhiannon and I had withdrawn to the Faerie Realms, I had seen Luna twice—once during Summer Solstice, when we held a remembrance ceremony in New Forest's town square, and once again at Winter Solstice, when we held a midwinter festival there.

Rhia and I had decided to make the holidays a recurring event. It would be a good way to keep the Fae Courts connected to the town, and involved in what was going on. We couldn't slide back into the old traditions of isolationism. That had led to disaster and vulnerability. But Luna… Luna and I had parted with strained emotions. Besides those two celebrations, I hadn't seen or heard from her.

"Please, show her in and bring another place setting." I glanced at Grieve, almost afraid. What if she was still furious at me? What if we would never be okay again?

And then, there she was, standing in the doorway. Luna, who was one of the yummanii—human. Luna, who was a bard, whose voice was her power. Her singing was brilliant and clear, scaling from soprano to alto depending on her whim. She could charm the birds with her song better than any Cinderella.

Luna, whom I had betrayed because I had no choice. Sometimes war leaves us no options.

Luna was short and curvy, slightly plump with hair down to her lower back. It was brunet, only she had streaked it with blond since I last saw her, reminding me of tiger stripes. Her eyes were the color of hot chocolate, ringed with silver from the magic she wove.

She had taken over the magic shop I had intended to run when I first returned to New Forest—Wind Charms. And she was now leader of the Moon Spinners, a coven that I had temporarily led. Even though I was a Wind witch—a powerful one—my ascension to the throne had precluded me from ever being a part of the outer world again in any discernible manner.

As she entered the room, dressed in a thick parka over a long skirt and warm sweater, she pulled off her gloves and let out a long sigh, her breath forming a mist as it escaped her lips. "You really can sit there with no coat, in just shirtsleeves?"

It was the first thing I had heard from her in months, but it might as well have been a hug. I laughed. "We have a fire going—we'll move the table next to it. Check, please?" I glanced at the guard and he nodded, instantly calling Fearless in to help him. I started, not expecting to see the guard back so soon.

"You're back from your family. How is…" I paused, not wanting to stir up worries, but I needed to know. If his mother had died, he would need time to mourn. As loyal as the guards were, personal tragedy always affected performance.

Fearless seemed to understand where I was going with my question. "Your Majesty, my mother passed. But I heard about the ship, and Check has filled me in on what happened at the shamans. I want to be here. I want to be useful. There's nothing I can do for my mother now, but at least here, I can make a difference."

The look on his face told me he needed to feel necessary. Death did that—death made a person want to wade in, to make a difference, because losing a loved one brought with it feelings of being out of control. I understood that all too well.

"You have my sympathy, Fearless. I'm truly sorry. You may return to your duties, but if you need time, please let us know. I have no problem with giving you mourning time." We stood back while they moved the table near the fire, and stoked up the flames. I motioned for them to seat Luna closest to the hearth. "Druise, please bring her a warm robe."

Druise dropped into a quick curtsey and dashed out of the room.

Luna tilted her head slightly, then laughed. "You've adapted to court life, Cicely. You may think you haven't, but you have." But there was no sarcasm in her voice, and I couldn't detect any hostility.

"I've had to." I paused while Druise returned with a warm dressing gown. "That will be less bulky, and actually warmer than your parka."

Luna handed her jacket to Druise and slipped the gown on. As she sat down again, she looked surprised. "You're right, it is."

She leaned back to allow the servant to fill her plate. We were having a thick stew, and hearty bread and sliced cheese and apple pie.

Then—"I imagine you are wondering why I'm here."

I stared at my plate, almost unable to breathe. "Yeah, actually. But…I've missed you. I'm glad you're here, for whatever reason."

Her lip twitched, but then she let out a long breath. "I came because I want you to know that I *do* understand why you did what you did. You hurt me. I felt so betrayed but, Cicely, I know things were desperate. I know how bad things were and how you had to absolutely have proof that we were loyal and not on Myst's side."

"Thank you." The words came out barely a whisper. I couldn't believe we were finally mending bridges.

"And I hope you understand that what I did, why I made the bargain with my ancestors—I wanted to make certain you know it wasn't a reaction to what happened. You weren't the only one terrified of what Myst was bringing to the table. My people—the yummanii—her Shadow Hunters were feeding on them, killing them. We were *all* in danger. We *all* had to do our part."

I nodded, slowly and sadly, the terror of those last days washing over me once again. Everything had happened so fast and in such a blur. It was one long, protracted nightmare. The blood had run so thick and free, the snow had been painted crimson.

"I ask you now, please, forgive me as much as you can. I never meant to unearth your secrets, especially for Kaylin to see them."

She closed her eyes and ducked her head. "Kaylin…" Then, looking up, she swallowed and I thought I saw the glimmer of tears in her eyes. "I miss him so much. I wish...I wish I hadn't been so afraid of who he was becoming."

"We all had our destinies to play out. I wonder where he is, and if he's all right."

"Sometimes, I feel him near me, Cicely. Sometimes, I think I can sense him outside my window...but when I look, there's no one there. I suppose we won't ever know." She let out a long sigh. "But to answer. Yes, I forgive you. I suppose, looking back, it's actually a good thing that I finally faced my memories. I've grown up a lot since then."

And then—the air cleared. The past seemed to recede. We could never go back, but we were here, on a new playing field, moving into the future.

"So, how are things in New Forest? I miss the Veil House. I miss the town." And it was then that I realized I was still homesick. I missed the only real home I had ever known.

"Rebuilding. The Shadow Hunters drove off so many people, but some are trickling back. Lannan and Regina are doing a great PR job on getting people to return." She paused over Lannan's name, eyeing me carefully. "Speaking of Lannan..."

I blushed. The vampire and I were still connected, and Grieve had come to accept it, but I had found a way to keep the peace.

"To answer your question, yes, Lannan and I still meet. We've agreed—two nights a year, on Midsummer and Midwinter. Who knows, it may peter itself out in the future. But in the end, he saved Grieve and he helped us destroy Myst. How can I turn my back on him now?"

She shrugged. "You can't, I suppose. But seriously, I'm

surprised by how well the vampires are persuading the yummanii to return. Though in an interesting twist, I'm noticing that mostly magic-born are moving to town, now."

"Really? That shifts the dynamics."

"Yes, and the New Forest Conservatory is starting to thrive. The school is branching out—the students are coming in droves. With the Consortium behind them, it's making a nationwide name for itself. For all the damage Myst did, everyone's coming together, in the end."

"Well, there's that. I wonder if New Forest won't grow bigger than it originally was, if the school is starting to thrive like you say."

"Wouldn't surprise me. There are some talented kids there. So, what's going on here?"

I glanced at Grieve, then decided that Luna should know about Fenrick. If he managed to cross through the portal into the Golden Wood, New Forest would be in danger.

"We have a new problem. I want you to talk to Ysandra about it, so the Consortium can prepare should things get out of hand. Also, I'll send word to Lannan and Regina." So I told her about Fenrick and the vargr and the Jötnar.

Luna paled. "One danger barely quashed and another rears its head. Please keep us informed. I'll talk to Ysandra when I get home tonight." She dug into her meal. "Delicious. You have great cooks."

"Coming from you, that's a compliment." Luna was an excellent cook. We chatted for a while, catching up, when Check once again peered inside the room after tapping on the door. His face looked strained.

"What is it, Check?" I sat down my fork.

"Your Majesty, we have a situation. It's the…it's Fenrick, Your Majesty. We've discovered where he is, and my men have also found the gateway."

I froze. "We need to move, then. Luna, I should send you home, but I worry about you traveling right now. I'm going to have to ask you to stay here until we deal with this."

She laughed. "I have my magic, I can make myself useful."

I shook my head. "I can't allow it. You'd be in danger if you come with us. I don't even know how we're going to do what we need to do." I couldn't imagine putting her through another battle—though when I thought about it, we were really on a decoy mission. To lure Fenrick back through the gateway, not to fight him. "Fenrick, as I told you, is a disgraced priest of Hel, and now he's fallen in with the frost giants."

"What are your goals?" She was suddenly all business, and a hardness flashed into her eyes that I didn't expect to see. "I've been working with my ancestors a lot over the past year. I might as well make the most of whatever time they allow me. My skills as a bard are very strong now."

I paused. "I wonder…could you charm a sorcerer? I can't imagine going up against his magic, but…" Quickly, I explained to her what we were trying to do. "We know we can't defeat him right now, but we have to lure him out. To drive him through the gate back into Jötunheim."

She frowned, concentrating. After a moment, she nodded. "I think…what are his triggers? What is he after?"

"As far as the shamans think, Fenrick is scouting ahead, foreshadowing the frost giants making a play to come through. From here, they can enter Midgard—the outer world—easier. I imagine they are thinking about setting off Ragnarök. If Fenrick can't grab power from the goddess of Death, this probably seems like the next best thing. So his triggers are power, and an assumption he can overtake the realm because I am new at this and not yet at my full power. This is an opportune time for them to attempt a push-through."

Luna contemplated. "His magic is that of snow and ice, and most likely death. He's going to be difficult to take on. I can charm, but I don't know whether he will have any resistance. Fire would be the best attack."

"We're not trying to attack him—we'll lose if we do. We're trying to bait him to return to the gate and then shove him through and seal it." Grieve frowned. "I wish the shamans would have been more specific."

"They aren't like the Internet, love. You can't just type in a question and get a clear answer." I shook my head. "They told us all they know."

"I know one way to draw him out, but it would be dangerous." Luna stared at me. "If he's after control of your realm, then you would be the best bait."

I glanced at her. That had been running through my mind. "Yeah, I was thinking along those same lines."

But the moment I spoke, Check was quick to pounce. "Your Majesty, absolutely not! You cannot entertain the thought. There is no way I can allow you to put yourself in danger like that."

Grieve surprised me, though. "I hate to agree, but in this case, Cicely and Luna are right. If he thinks he has a chance to take down the Crown, he'll go for it. He's drawing on the spirits from *The Wave Catcher*. He's not going to let the chance to absorb the Queen's powers slip away. He's power hungry. I doubt the frost giants realize how thirsty he is. They probably think they're using him, while he thinks he's using them."

"Well, they're both getting something out of it, at least." Luna snorted. She turned to Check. "I know you're worried about Cicely, but seriously, she's your best hope to luring him out. What else are you going to do? What else could he possibly want unless you offer to open up the door and let him just waltz in with his buddies?"

"She's right," I said. "The only other option is to seal the gate with him over here. But if we can't take him down, there is nothing that can stop him from creating another gate back into Jötunheim, is there?" Which begged the question—once we shoved him back through, how long before he tried again? I shook off the thought. *Deal with one problem at a time.*

"I wish Kaylin was around. He seemed to have a strong connection for coping with spirits and the like. He might be able to figure out how to stop Fenrick from feeding on life force." For the second time that day, remorse filled Luna's voice.

I rested my hand on her shoulder. "You really did love him, didn't you?"

She shrugged. "There's no use in dwelling on it. What's done is done. I lost him long ago, when his night-veil demon woke up and took over, I would have lost him anyway."

Check had been listening. He was obviously unhappy with the turn in conversation, but finally he said, "I suppose you are right. But we do this cautiously. We set you up near the gate. We make certain you are as protected as we can without giving ourselves away."

"Strict is going to blow a gasket." I almost laughed. As much as I had grown to like my chief advisor, I still got a kick out of crossing him on occasion. He had pushed me so hard on my studies to assimilate, and he had been so unrelenting, it gave me a snarky thrill when I was able to catch him off guard.

"Leave him to me." Grieve stood. "I'll be back. We have to move fast. We have the Flammen in Court, so we can make the necessary preparations." Without another word, Grieve headed toward the door. Check and Fearless withdrew outside the room, and Druise took a quiet spot across the room, minding her own business as she mended the train of one of my dresses that I had caught in a door.

Luna and I were alone. I walked over to her and held out my arms. She slid into them, hugging me tightly. We both were teary-eyed.

"I've missed you, my friend." I finally found my voice. "I've missed talking to you. I love my life, I love Grieve and my place here, but it gets lonely. And I miss my cousin. I miss my friends. You and Peyton…and I miss Kaylin too."

We walked, hand in hand, to the chaise next to the fireplace where we sat, holding our hands out to the flames. I wasn't cold at all, but Luna was still shivering. She stared at the fire, transfixed, while I stared at her.

"You know," she said, still absorbed by the flames, "when I made the deal with Dorthea, I knew we would win. I just knew it."

"Are you afraid, knowing they could come for you at any time?" I wasn't sure how to phrase it—how far to pry.

But she had opened the door and I was willing to walk in, if she needed to talk about it.

Luna looked over at me. "You remember when Peyton's father was killed? How quick it was and how none of us were expecting it?"

I nodded. We had watched a vampire named Geoffrey take down Rex, Peyton's father, as we exited a dress shop when Rhiannon and I were shopping for wedding dresses. It had been sudden, brutal, and totally unexpected.

"I do."

"I remember thinking right then, nothing is guaranteed. Nobody knows how long they have in this world. With the evils that are out there, and the accidents that can happen... Nobody gets out alive, Cicely. *You* may live for a thousand...two thousand years. Or, you might slip on the ice and crack your head and be dead by tomorrow."

"I was thinking about this not long ago."

"It's the nature of life. So when I realized the price I'd have to pay for Dorthea's help, I thought about all the people Myst killed. I thought about Rex...I thought about everything that had happened. And I realized that whether my ancestors come to claim me, or an accident, or a vampire's fangs—one way or another, *I'm going to die someday*. I decided I wanted to choose how, and in doing so, do something good for the world." She sounded almost cheerful.

She made sense. A fatalistic view that wasn't mopey. "We have what time we have, I guess." Reaching out, I squeezed her hand. "I'm just glad we're friends again."

"Me, too." Luna smiled.

The door opened at that moment and Grieve strode in, followed by Check and Fearless. "We're ready. The

Flammen will meet us along the way. Our men know where Fenrick is and they will make *certain* he overhears them talk about the fact that you're going to personally oversee the investigation of the gateway to Jötunheim. Then, we have to pray he takes the bait."

I stood. "I'll get dressed." Turning to Luna, I added, "Are you sure you want to come with us? It may be dangerous."

She laughed. "What have I got to lose? My life is already forfeit. I doubt the ancestors will let a sorcerer-priest kill me before they get the chance."

And with that, we were in motion, ready to hunt the hunter.

CHAPTER SIX

W e were on our way. Luna wasn't geared for our weather so Check broke out a sledge and I rode in it with her, a thick blanket bundled around us.

The sleigh was pulled by Ice Elementals in the shape of horses, translucent and glistening against the snow. After we had defeated Myst, the wonders of this realm started becoming clear. I hadn't realized that Ice Elementals could change their shape. In fact, I had no clue what their normal shape was. Some pristine, ice blue flame, I supposed. All flickering with the energy of the primal winter. Now, though, they were crystalline stallions, pulling the sledge without tiring.

Luna's gaze was fastened on them, amazement filling her eyes.

"I never knew there could be so much beauty. You love living here, don't you," she asked, and I heard a wistful sigh in her voice. "I wish there was a place I felt at home. Don't get me wrong, I love the Veil House, but it's not really mine. Having Peyton there helps, though. We get along really well."

"Did your parents ever find out about Zoey?" I knew I was touching on a volatile subject, but I might as well get it over with.

In a soft voice, Luna whispered, "No. Oh, they know she's dead, but I told them it was a car accident. I told them she skidded off the road due to the ice, and that she died instantly when she hit a tree. When I took her body home after we killed Myst, I had her cremated. I sent them her ashes. I couldn't have them with me—not after what she did. But I thought my parents needed closure and they'd never have if I told them the truth."

I nodded. There was nothing else to say. Zoey had betrayed us, though we could never be certain it was her fault. And in the end, she had paid with her life.

As we traveled toward the gate, the sky darkened. Night came early in our realm, and I leaned back against the seat, my head resting against Luna's shoulder. She took my hand in hers. The rift between us vanished for good in that simplest of touches.

I pointed to the sky, where the aurora borealis shimmered in a way that it never did back through the portal. In our realm, the lights lit up the sky, sparkling and dancing from one end of the horizon to the other — ripples of blue and green and purple, swirls of red and pink and golden shimmers. And it crackled. You could hear the sparks dancing until the whole sky seemed ablaze with energy.

Luna caught her breath. She shook her head as she stared into the night. "I have never seen anything quite so beautiful. In some ways, I envy you, Cicely. I don't envy you your throne or the responsibilities you have, but to live in a place like this… I would think you could never forget about the magic inherent within the world. Not here."

Her words stopped me short. Though there was truth to them, I realized that I had been taking this beauty for granted more and more. Perhaps that was inevitable, no matter where one lived—getting so used to one's surroundings that it no longer seemed brilliant and beautiful. I decided right there to try and find a little wonder in every day.

Check was jogging alongside the sleigh. He laughed and waved at the aurora. "The gods look down from heaven tonight. Sometimes I wish that I could go across the Bifrost bridge instead of to the Golden Isle when my time comes."

"How much further till we get there?" I was starting to get tired.

"We're close now, Your Majesty. Almost there." His joy vanished into somberness and he went ahead to talk to Captain Shell.

Luna straightened her shoulders. "I'll do my best to prepare a spell to charm the sorcerer. I don't know if it will work, but I doubt it could hurt. It never does harm to have a backup plan and if nothing else, the magic should throw him off guard."

A few moments later, Grieve, Captain Shell, and Check returned. Check pointed to the stand of trees ahead. The fir towered over the land, a thicket blotting out the field beyond.

"On the other side of the copse. That's where the gate lies. Now we just have to hope Fenrick took the bait. The

Flammen is ready, and seems eager to help. He's been fully briefed in the order of how to destroy the runes." The guard paused, then added, "You know, Your Majesty, until you took the throne, we had little to do with the Wilding Fae. And they wanted little to do with us. You have brought our people together in a way that no one could predict."

"I think perhaps that's what Rhiannon and I are meant to do. We are neither fully Cambyra Fae, nor fully magic-born. We stand between worlds and now, we pull worlds together." And right then I understood the logic of Lainule and Wrath when they set into motion their plan. Rhiannon and I were pawns, created for a very necessary strategy.

"We should go on foot from here. However, I fear the Lady Luna will not be able to walk atop the snow. One of our men will carry her on his back." Captain Shell reached up to help us down from the sledge.

Luna shook her head. "I'm too heavy. I don't want to hurt anyone."

Check laughed, but kindly. "Lady Luna, you are a mere slip to us. The Cambyra are extremely strong, and you are not the weight you think you are. Have no fear, you will neither harm nor hinder us."

He motioned to one of the guards who immediately hustled over. I recognized him as Chasing. He was so named because he liked to run everywhere, and was faster than most of his compatriots. He had a shock of brilliant blond hair that stood out among the mostly dark-haired Winter Fae. It was not so platinum as Grieve's, but was as golden as the sun. I had a feeling his parentage was at least partly from the Summer Court.

Check introduced Chasing to Luna. "You will carry the Lady Luna through the copse to the very edge and wait there for us. Take two other men to help guard her."

Chasing knelt so that Luna could climb on his back. She giggled, blushing ever so slightly, but did as he bade. As he stood up, adjusting her weight and holding her legs around him, he whispered something to her and she laughed again, this time her cheeks flaming. I trusted my guards to be polite, so I figured that whatever he said had struck her as slightly risqué but not offensive.

She flashed a look to me. "If you had told me this morning that I would be riding the back of one of the Cambyra Fae in the Court of Snow and Ice, I would have called you crazy. Yet, here I am."

I waved as the guard carried her off into the copse. "Now what?"

Check glanced at Grieve and Captain Shell. "Now, we follow them."

Before we could start, another guard ran over to us. He knelt, inclining his head. "Your Majesty, we have word that the sorcerer Fenrick is headed this way. He over-heard our guards—as was our plan—and immediately set out in this direction. He moves quickly and is surrounded by a dozen of the vargr. They look hungry, Your Majesty, and dangerous."

"We must move," Check said. "Fenrick can move as fast as the wind and he will be here soon. We weren't sure if he would take the bait, but apparently the thought of finding you out here is too tempting. We must be ready."

One of the guards stayed behind to hide the sledge and the horses as the rest of us headed toward the trees.

Before long, we were in the heart of the thicket, beside Luna and her guards.

As we stood next to a tree covered with low-growing branches, Check motioned for us to look between the limbs. There, not ten yards from where we were standing, stood a glowing archway. As in the vision that I had experienced back with the shamans, a ripple of energy filled the arch from top to bottom and side to side. It crackled and snapped. There was something evil about this gateway, I could feel it even from where we stood. It was dark and foreboding, filled with anger and chaos and destruction all rolled into one. If this was a sample of what awaited on the other side, we couldn't let the frost giants from Jötunheim enter our realm.

Grieve breathed softly beside me. "Can you feel it? I thought Myst the most dangerous creature ever alive, but what lies beyond that gateway could easily rival Myst and the Indigo Court."

I rested a hand on his arm, more to reassure myself than for balance. "I can feel it. Whatever lies beyond the gate seethes with hunger for power and destruction. Do you think we brought enough guards with us?"

"I hope so." Grieve motioned to Check. "Do we have enough manpower? If there are a dozen vargr coming with him, do you think we can fight them?"

His gaze firmly fastened on the gateway, Check slowly nodded. "I believe we can if we don't have to fight Fenrick as well. The trick will be to push him through. I have talked to the Flammen and he is ready to move on our mark. Your Majesty?" He turned to me, a drawn look on his face. "I cannot believe I am about to say this, but you must walk out and stand near the gate. We will be ready to rush in to protect you. I still think this is folly, but if you must do this, I beg of you to be prepared to change shape. Fly away as quickly as possible. You cannot outrun the sorcerer, but you can outfly him, I believe."

I sucked in a deep breath. Even though it would be difficult to kill me, the possibility was still there and I didn't entertain the thought of being a sorcerer's plaything. But having felt the energy of the gate, I knew this was the only thing we could do.

"I'm ready. I will be ready to transform into my owl shape at the first sign of trouble."

"No, wait for our mark. The moment you change shape and fly away, we'll rush in. If we take him by surprise, we can drive him through the gate and then the Flammen will immediately target the runes. If we can injure him in the process, so much the better."

"I'll stand to this side of the gate, then. That way I won't be in the way. But the vargr will be with him, and your men will be caught up in fighting them. You should assign two or three to focus on Fenrick while the rest take on the wild wolves."

Luna spoke up. She had shuffled her way over to us and was attempting to stand on the crust of snow without breaking through. "The moment I see him I will begin my spell. In fact, if I step out along with Cicely—pardon me, the Queen—it may distract him long enough for your men to run in. Especially if I am actively casting a spell at that time. He won't be expecting me and he won't know what to think."

Check smiled broadly. "No one can ever tell me that the yummanii aren't courageous. Nor that women can't be as fierce as any warrior man."

Luna bobbed her head at him, smiling back. "Trust me, Check, when you have very little left to lose, fear ceases to be much of a factor. My life is forfeit and I have no idea when I will be forced to pay the price. So if I can help out, why not go out with a blaze?" She turned to me. "Tell me when."

From the distance we heard a terrible baying, it filled the air—howls and yips and snarls that echoed from the distance. As the cacophony grew louder, I drew a deep breath and kissed Grieve. "I love you. *Promise me* you'll be careful, because I know you will be out there fighting with the others. And I promise to fly away as soon as I see him coming toward me." It was the only way I could ease both our minds.

He nodded, kissing me back. "So, it would seem we are not done with our battles yet."

"And this…this is no battle, but I fear it is quite probably the predecessor to one."

At that moment Check gave me a nod. "Now, Your Majesty."

As I stepped out into the open, Luna followed behind me, trudging knee-deep in the snow. In the near distance we could see a blur of smoke and shadow. The vargr, racing at the helm, and behind them their lord and master —Fenrick.

Even from this distance I could see him. He was burly and tall, taller than any man I had ever seen. He towered like a giant himself. His hair was black as night, his skin pale as frost—he might have been a vampire for the pallor in his cheeks. Robed in gray furs, he traversed the snow faster than the Cambyra could run. He ran with the storm behind him, with boiling clouds in his wake and a flurry of snow that surrounded him. In front of him the vargr raced. Gigantic wolves, they were dark and vicious and there was a glint in their eyes that spoke of evil rather than animal instinct. These were no wolves of our realm. They were shades, shadows from Jötunheim, and they were out for blood.

Luna began to sing, loud and clear in a voice that echoed across the plain. The notes spiraled up, powerful and strong, and by just their sound, I realized how far she had advanced in her magic. As she stood near me, I gathered my power and raised my arms overhead.

"You are not welcome in my realm!" I cast my voice ahead of me to echo through the plain, rolling like thunder.

As he closed in, Fenrick laughed. "Your realm will soon be my realm, oh Faerie Queen of the night. You may be the Queen of Winter, but you are not the Queen of Frost." He raised one hand and gathered to him a ball of energy that circled his wrist. It grew, blue and white sparking off of the purple.

Quickly I shifted, transforming into my owl shape. Hands to feathers, arms to wings, lengthening and spreading out into the great barred owl that I was. I flew up, gliding on the currents heading toward the forest. I wanted to stay and fight, but I had promised, and my decisions were not my own now. The Queen does not compromise her own safety.

Below me, Luna continued to sing. As I glanced back, Fenrick paused, staring at her, a look of confusion on his face. In that moment, my men raced out of the woods, three of them heading directly toward the sorcerer.

The others engaged the vargr and the fight was on.

Grieve attacked one of the shadow wolves. It snapped at him, and he shifted into his own Wolf shape, meeting it snarl for snarl, snap for snap, bite for bite. They wrestled as I shifted back into myself, balancing on one of the limbs in the tall fir nearest the action. I cringed as the vargr's muzzle closed in on Grieve's throat. At that moment Check rushed in, thrusting his sword into the wolf's side, pinning it to the ground. The vargr dropped and Grieve moved on to engage the next, Check by his side. They worked as a pair even as my other men faced their snarling opponents.

The three men who descended on Fenrick grabbed hold of him and the ball of energy he had been amassing went wild, skidding to the side. It almost hit Luna, but she rolled out of the way, falling into the snow beside the gate.

I had a sudden fear that they wouldn't be able to handle him—he was throwing them off. So, raising my arms, I whispered the words, *Twister.*

No, Cicely—you can't.

Ulean, I have to do something.

She fell silent, and I focused on the power of the wind. It started slowly, but suddenly sprang up to surround me —a whirling mass of wind, sweeping snow and branch and bough into its vortex. I rose up atop it, riding it like a mighty ship, driving it forward toward Fenrick.

My men knew enough to scramble out of the way, though I heard Grieve scream out my name. But in the moment, the fury of the storm raged through me and I leaned my head back, laughing. The desire to let go, to become part of the storm, wrestled with my conscious thoughts, but I struggled to keep control, straining to force the tornado to bend to my command. Storms were capricious and had their own agendas, but I could control this—I knew I could.

Forcing the whirling dervish of a storm toward Fenrick, I bore down on him, laughing like a maniac, thrilling to the power as the storm raged through my soul.

He whirled, eyes wide. He had obviously not expected a tornado to greet him. I drove the storm forward and he began to back up as I came near enough to catch him up in the winds. He turned to scramble away, leaping in giant strides across the snow toward the gate.

Relieved to see that the guards had pulled Luna out of the way, I forced myself to release the twister, aiming it at him, and I fell toward the ground, sweeping up in my owl form at the last moment.

Fenrick paused long enough to shout something—the winds drowned it out for anyone with normal hearing but I could hear him, in the slipstream. "I'll be back, and I'll tear your kingdom to shreds." Then he leaped once, disappearing through the gateway. The tornado siphoned through after him.

Immediately, the Flammen, who had been standing to the side, rushed up to direct his flame toward the runes. It emerged from his eye—that single brilliant glowing eye of his. The fire pierced the runes and they melted away at its touch. First one rune, then another, and the third, and then they were gone. The gate creaked and groaned, shattering into a million ice shards.

The vargr continued to fight, staining the snow crimson as they died. And then, there was silence. The immediate threat was over.

THREE OF OUR men were still as ice, lying in frozen pools of blood on the ground. I returned to my normal form and knelt beside them, praying they were still alive.

One—a young man whom I knew was a new father—was dead. No breath rose from his chest. I grabbed his wrist and felt for a pulse but he was done. I would have tried CPR, except I happened to glance down at his chest. The vargr had slashed a hole in him, ripping him open from one side to the other. I quietly placed his arm back on the snow and turned to see how the others were faring. One was seriously wounded, his leg cut open, but Fearless was applying a tourniquet and told me he would live. The third was also dead.

I stared at the place where the gate had stood. Fenrick's last words echoed in my head. We weren't done with him yet. It was personal now. But for the moment, we would tend to our wounded and dead.

The snow was covered with blood. It had melted in little rivulets through the field, then froze to form sparkling crimson fingers.

"He'll be coming back, won't he?" Luna followed my gaze as she picked herself up off the ground. She did her best to balance on the snow and one of the guards moved over to lend her an arm. She thanked him and he smiled at her.

I didn't want to answer. But it was better to face reality than live in blind hope. "Yes. It's personal now. And he knows that even with my ability to summon a storm, we are vulnerable. We barely fought off the vargr. If I hadn't chased him through the gateway with that tornado, chances are good we'd all be dead."

"Your Majesty…you must… Never mind." Check

looked up from where he was attending to the wounded guard. The tourniquet had stopped the bleeding. Fearless was doing what he could to fashion a stretcher. But even I could see that the guard's life still hung in the balance.

"I think this might have been a test run. I wonder how long we have. The frost giants will question him, and he will tell them everything he has learned. He has seen our strengths, but more important, I think he realizes we are still weak. The moment we get home to the Barrow, we need to begin planning. I fear there is war coming. Whether it be tomorrow or in twenty years, no one can say. But we can't allow ourselves to grow complacent."

The wind picked up and Ulean was suddenly there, gusting around me.

You must learn to harness the power of the wind now. You could be such a formidable opponent if you can gain control over it. Do not forget this moment, Cicely. The gods have long memories, and the giants might as well be gods. I doubt if they will be back quickly—but it cannot hurt to prepare.

I rather hoped we were done with war.

No kingdom is ever done with war. There will always be an enemy at the gate. There will always be an enemy looking to take over the kingdom. This is as true in the realm of Snow and Ice as it is in the yummanii realm.

I motioned to Captain Shell. "The wounded man can ride in the sledge with Luna. I can easily run back to the Barrow with the rest of you."

"Very well, Your Majesty. Thank you. It will increase his chances of survival."

And so we turned and, leaving the vargr where they had fallen, we headed back home for the Barrow. But my thoughts were deep in a battle I knew would come. I only hoped we had time to prepare and to strengthen our forces.

✳

LUNA STAYED THE NIGHT, and though our talk turned away from Fenrick to focus on friends and old times, we both seemed to realize that—though we were friends again— we had our separate lives to lead. After a couple glasses of wine she sighed and sat down hers.

"I'm glad I came. I'm glad I went with you and saw the reality of what's out there. In some ways, I wish I could just leave and think, *Oh, this is Cicely's problem, not mine.* But really, the problem belongs to all of us. The world is so much bigger than I ever thought it was. I'll talk to Ysandra and the Consortium tomorrow…tell them about the threat. We will do what we can on our side to prepare, just in case they break through next time. We may live in different worlds, but we face common enemies."

The next day, after Luna left, Grieve and I met with Strict, Captain Shell, and Thorn.

We began hammering out a strategy for when Fenrick would return. At one point, I crossed to the fireplace. As I stared into the glowing flames, it hit me: *This* is what it meant to be Queen. This is what it meant to be responsible for the lives of my people. Strategies and war, battle plans and preparations. They were as important as protecting my people against hunger and illness. Like it or not, to be leader meant being a warrior.

Grieve approached, resting a hand on my shoulder. "What are you thinking?"

I shook my head. "I'm thinking…I feel so much older

than I did a year ago. It feels like my life before I returned to New Forest never even existed. Sometimes I wonder if my life outside was all a dream, and I just woke up here, where I've always been."

"You were thrust into a life you never expected. Are you sorry that you rescued Lainule's heartstone? In doing so, you sealed both her fate and yours."

I thought about his question. If I had not saved Lainule's life, I would not have necessarily had to accept my destiny. She had warned me as much as she could.

"Do you understand what you are offering? No, you do not."

"I'm offering to try to save your life."

"No, Cicely. You offer so much more than that— you make a sacrifice if you choose to do this and I cannot tell you just what that is. Not yet."

The memory of that meeting rang in my mind. If I hadn't rescued her heartstone, Lainule would have died. And the realm of Rivers and Rushes would have faded, fair game for whomever might take it for themselves.

I shook my head. "I don't regret what I did. Destiny would have played out anyway, but it could easily have been Myst's destiny. She might have been able to take full control and spin out her plans to her end goal."

I turned and placed my hands on his shoulders, staring into his eyes. I loved my Fae Prince. I had loved him as long as I could remember.

"To be your wife, to be Queen to your King, it is worth all we have been through and all that is to come. I would choose no other path. Come frost giants and vargr, come enemies we have not yet met… As long as I can be by your side, that is all that matters. We will have children and grandchildren, and we will rule this realm with justice and love. This is our home, and we will keep it safe together."

He leaned down and pressed his lips against mine and in that moment, any regrets I might have still had slipped away. For the first time since I had taken the throne, I truly felt like I belonged here.

❋

IF YOU ENJOYED this book in my Indigo Court Series and want to read the entire series, you will find them available for your e-reader: NIGHT MYST, NIGHT VEIL, NIGHT SEEKER, NIGHT VISION, and NIGHT'S END.

You might also enjoy my new series The Wild Hunt. Darker urban fantasy/paranormal romance, the first four books are out: THE SILVER STAG, OAK & THORNS, IRON BONES, A SHADOW OF CROWS, and THE HALLOWED HUNT. The sixth, THE SILVER MIST, will be out in a couple of months.

I also invite you to visit Fury's world. In a gritty, post-apocalyptic Seattle, Fury is a minor goddess, in charge of eliminating the Abominations who come off the World Tree. Book 1-5 are available now in the Fury Unbound Series : FURY RISING, FURY'S MAGIC, FURY AWAK-ENED, FURY CALLING, and FURY'S MANTLE.

If you prefer a lighter-hearted but still steamy para-normal romance, meet the wild and magical residents of Bedlam in my Bewitching Bedlam Series. Fun-loving witch Maddy Gallowglass, her smoking-hot vampire lover Aegis, and their crazed cjinn Bubba (part djinn, all cat) rock it out in Bedlam, a magical town on a magical island. BLOOD MUSIC, BEWITCHING BEDLAM,

MAUDLIN'S MAYHEM, SIREN'S SONG, WITCHES WILD, CASTING CURSES, BLOOD VENGEANCE, TIGER TAILS, and Bubba's origin story THE WISH FACTOR are all available.

If you like cozies with teeth, try my Chintz 'n China paranormal mysteries. The series is complete with: GHOST OF A CHANCE, LEGEND OF THE JADE DRAGON, MURDER UNDER A MYSTIC MOON, A HARVEST OF BONES, ONE HEX OF A WEDDING, and a wrap-up novella: HOLIDAY SPIRITS.

The newest Otherworld book—HARVEST SONG—is available now, and the last, BLOOD BONDS, will be available in April 2019.

For all of my work, both published and upcoming releases, see the Biography at the end of this book, or check out my website at Galenorn.com and be sure and sign up for my newsletter to receive news about all my new releases.

CHARACTER LIST

CICELY AND THE COURT OF SNOW AND ICE

- **Captain Shell:** Captain of the Court of Snow and Ice's military guard.
- **Check:** Cicely's personal guard
- **Cicely Waters:** A witch who can control the wind. One of the magic-born and half Uwilahsidhe (the Owl people of the Cambyra Fae). Born on the Summer Solstice at midnight, a daughter of the Moon/Waning Year. The new Queen of Snow and Ice.
- **Druise:** Cicely's lady's maid
- **Fearless:** Cicely's personal guard
- **Flammen:** One of the Wilding Fae, from the village of Whitecroft.
- **Grieve:** (*See also* Indigo Court) King of the Court of Snow and Ice. One of the Cambyra Fae (shapeshifting Fae) now turned Vampiric Fae. Obsessed and in love with Cicely.

- **Hunter:** Cicely's grandfather. Wrath's father.
- **Silverweb:** The treasurer of the Court of Snow and Ice
- **Snow Hag:** One of the Wilding Fae. A friend of Cicely's.
- **Strict:** Cicely's chief advisor
- **Tabera:** The late Queen of Snow and Ice

RHIANNON AND THE COURT OF RIVERS AND RUSHES

- **Chatter:** King of the Summer Court. Grieve's best friend.
- **Edge:** Rhiannon's Court Advisor
- **Lainule:** The former Fae Queen of Rivers and Rushes. Grieve's aunt and Rhiannon's aunt. The former Queen of Summer. Returned to the Golden Isle.
- **Rhiannon Roland:** Cicely's cousin, born on the same day as Cicely, only at daybreak, a daughter of the Sun / Waxing Year. Rhiannon is also half Cambyra Fae, and half magic-born, and she controls the power of fire. The new Queen of Rivers and Rushes.
- **Wrath:** Cicely's father—one of the Uwilahsidhe and originally a member of the Court of Snow and Ice (the Owl people of the Cambyra Fae)

PEYTON AND THE COURT OF THE MAGIC-BORN

- **Anadey:** Traitor; was a friend of Heather's and

mentor to Rhiannon. One of the magic-born, Anadey can work with all elements. Peyton's mother. Deceased.

- **Kaylin Chen:** Martial arts sensei, a dreamwalker, has a night-veil demon merged into his soul.
- **Luna Saunders:** Yummanii bard
- **Peyton MoonRunner:** Half werepuma, half magic-born. Anadey's daughter.
- **Rex MoonRunner:** Werepuma. Peyton's father. Deceased.
- **Ysandra Petros:** Member of the Consortium. Yummanii and powerful witch who can control sound, energy, and force.

THE INDIGO COURT

- **Myst:** Queen of the Indigo Court, mother of the Vampiric Fae, the Mistress of Mayhem. Queen of Winter.
- **Heather Roland:** (*See also* Indigo Court) Rhiannon's mother and Cicely's aunt. One of the magic-born, an herbalist, first turned into a vampire by the Indigo Court, now truly dead.

THE VEIN LORDS/TRUE VAMPIRES

- **Crawl:** The Blood Oracle: One of the oldest Vein Lords, made by the Crimson Queen herself. Sire to Regina and Lannan.
- **Geoffrey:** Former NW Regent of the Vampire

Nation and one of the Elder Vein Lords. 2,000 years old, from Xiongnu. Truly Dead.

- **Lannan Altos:** Professor at the New Forest Conservatory, Elder vampire, brother and lover to Regina Altos, hedonistic golden boy. New NW Regent of the Vampire Nation.
- **Leo Bryne:** Was Rhiannon's fiancé, a healer and one of the magic-born. Leo was a day-runner for Geoffrey, turned to a vampire by Geoffrey. Deceased.
- **Regina Altos:** Emissary for the Crimson Court / Queen. Originally from Sumer with her brother and lover, Lannan. Was a priestess of Inanna. Turned by Crawl.

BIOGRAPHY

New York Times, Publishers Weekly, and USA Today
bestselling author Yasmine Galenorn writes urban fantasy
and paranormal romance, and is the author of over sixty
books, including the Wild Hunt Series, the Fury Unbound
Series, the Bewitching Bedlam Series, the Indigo Court
Series, and the Otherworld Series, among others. She's
also written nonfiction metaphysical books. She is the
2011 Career Achievement Award Winner in Urban
Fantasy, given by RT Magazine.

Yasmine has been in the Craft since 1980, is a
shamanic witch and High Priestess. She describes her life
as a blend of teacups and tattoos. She lives in Kirkland,
WA, with her husband Samwise and their cats. Yasmine
can be reached via her website at Galenorn.com.

Indie Releases Currently Available:

The Wild Hunt Series:

The Silver Stag
Oak & Thorns
Iron Bones
A Shadow of Crows
The Hallowed Hunt
The Silver Mist

Bewitching Bedlam Series:
Bewitching Bedlam
Maudlin's Mayhem
Siren's Song
Witches Wild
Casting Curses
Blood Music
Blood Vengeance
Tiger Tails
The Wish Factor

Fury Unbound Series:
Fury Rising
Fury's Magic
Fury Awakened
Fury Calling
Fury's Mantle

Indigo Court Series:
Night Myst
Night Veil
Night Seeker
Night Vision
Night's End

Night Shivers

Otherworld Series:
Moon Shimmers
Harvest Song
Blood Bonds
Earthbound
Knight Magic
Otherworld Tales: Volume One
Tales From Otherworld: Collection One
Men of Otherworld: Collection One
Men of Otherworld: Collection Two
Moon Swept: Otherworld Tales of First Love
For the rest of the Otherworld Series, see website at
Galenorn.com.

Chintz 'n China Series:
Ghost of a Chance
Legend of the Jade Dragon
Murder Under a Mystic Moon
A Harvest of Bones
One Hex of a Wedding
Holiday Spirits

Bath and Body Series (originally under the name India Ink):
Scent to Her Grave
A Blush With Death
Glossed and Found

Misc. Short Stories/Anthologies:

The Longest Night: A Starwood Novella
Mist and Shadows: Tales From Dark Haunts
Once Upon a Kiss (short story: Princess Charming)
Once Upon a Curse (short story: Bones)

Magickal Nonfiction:
Embracing the Moon
Tarot Journeys

30094771R00078

Printed in Great
Britain
by Amazon